Lyons opened  with a choice

Double-ought and number-two balls spewed out of the Atchisson as Lyons moved on toward the back wall.

When he reached the wall he put his fist through it. Within seconds he had punched and kicked his way through the plasterboard.

Now he was in the computer room. Lyons's right hand went to his hip and came back filled with Colt Python.

The Python destroyed each head whose body held a gun.

Stunned survivors stared at the crazy man as he continued his advance, Colt and Atchisson in debating position. . . .

But who in hell wants to argue with Carl Lyons!

Mack Bolan's

ABLE TEAM

Mack Bolan's

PHOENIX FORCE

ABLE TEAM
Deathbites

Dick Stivers

A GOLD EAGLE BOOK FROM
W☉RLDWIDE

TORONTO · NEW YORK · LONDON · PARIS
AMSTERDAM · STOCKHOLM · HAMBURG
ATHENS · MILAN · TOKYO · SYDNEY

First edition June 1984

ISBN 0-373-61212-5

Special thanks and acknowledgment to Tom Arnett
for his contributions to this work.

Printed in Canada

1

June 1, 1520 hours, Osaka, Japan

Dr. Uemurea knelt beside the low table in one corner of his office, his untasted tea in front of him. He touched the stout white-oak stick he always carried and looked at Aya Jishin who knelt opposite him. She was explaining how Japan could *overcome* American competition in computer development. She explained hoarsely, fervently and urgently.

Uemurea knew he would have to kill her.

He looked attentively at this woman, his face carefully impassive. Behind the mask of polite intentness, he let his mind wander. Again he touched the stick; he had great faith in it.

Uemurea was Japan's top computer researcher, but to him technology was only a thing of the mind; it meant nothing to the soul. Uemurea's soul yearned to observe the old ways, to once again find the glory that had been Japan's in past centuries. So, he had a traditional tea table in one corner of his office, while all his colleagues had American chrome clutter. Every day he went to the dojo to practice *bojitsu*, the deadly art of the staff, while others at the research facility collected pulled muscles playing squash and racquetball.

Then this creature, this Aya Jishin, had come to him with a repulsive proposition. She knew he would refuse, refuse curtly, and that could only mean she did not intend to let him live to repeat that proposition to anyone else.

He looked at the hands of Aya Jishin—blunt fingers, huge ridges of calluses. They were ugly, deformed hands that had been plunged again and again into beans, rice, sand until they were little better than maces on the end of her muscular arms. The arms swung from wide shoulders.

Whatever this thing kneeling, facing him was, it was not a woman. The bland, expressionless face, the perfect dark eyes, were not meant to be accented by a nose that had been improperly reset and a cauliflower ear. Suddenly it occurred to him that he was looking at the type of Japanese woman he pretended to honor. In the past, the samurai women had fought as well as the men. Some had been extremely proficient warriors. Was this repulsive creature actually a throwback to the times he wished he had lived?

He shook off the dreadful notion, at the same time mechanically shaking his head. He was not aware that he had shaken his head until Aya Jishin stopped in mid-sentence, respectfully waiting for him to voice his objection.

The scientist found himself reluctant to state his view. It was not that he did not know the only course permitted by honor, it was just that he suddenly felt his fifty years and did not look forward to the exertion of physical violence. A workout was one thing, actually having to fight for one's life was something else.

Dr. Uemurea was just opening his mouth to speak when there was shouting and screaming from outside his office. He rose quickly, perturbed by the nature of the sound, but thankful for the interruption. Across the table, Jishin rose smoothly, easily.

"It is the New Red Brigade," she said. "We are destroying this place." Her speech was still quiet, her voice still hoarse, but the speech form had changed from a person speaking to a superior to a person speaking to an inferior.

"You never expected me to go along with your plan," Uemurea said.

She shook her large head. "No, but your research will put the plan into operation. You deserved the right to refuse."

The scientist was amazed by the cultural correctness of her action. In a flash of insight, Uemurea realized that while he had been romanticizing about Japan's past, this terrorist had been living it.

"What is happening out there?" he casually asked, leaning on his cane.

"The workers are being killed so they can identify no one. The electronic files and the paper files will then be loaded into trucks. As I explained, we must use them if we are to defeat the Americans in computer sales."

"But you're not really interested in who sells the most or the best computers, no more than I am."

She shrugged. "Not computers, as opposed to cars, televisions, or anything else. But the ability to manufacture is power. Being able to manufacture the best is more power. I am interested in that."

"Thank you for your honesty. Then you really think you can speed the disintegration of America?"

She grinned, an ugly gap-toothed grin. "I shall bring about that downfall, myself. First, they will lose their computer researchers, then other researchers, then those who manufacture things."

"And where will a disfigured Nipponese like yourself be able to hide in the United States?" he scornfully bated her. "You'll stand out like one of their neon signs would stand out in one of our temples."

"I'll be safe within WAR," she replied.

Uemurea attacked. One moment his hands were idly toying with the *jo*, the breaker of swords, the next moment it was whistling at her head with skull-crushing force.

Aya Jishin moved her clenched fists together to form one elongated fist. Her movements were perfectly executed. The mountainous ridge of hardened knuckles suddenly was in the path of the striking stick. With a crack like a high-powered rifle, the seasoned oak broke over the knuckles. Half the stick spun away, burying itself in the plaster of the office wall. The other half stung Uemurea's hand. He let it drop and it rolled behind him. Uemurea turned sideways, exposing fewer vital areas to those pile-driving fists. His arms came up to protect throat and face, elbows in to protect the upper body.

Jishin grinned and struck his forearms with a lightning left-right. The scientist could hear the bones in his forearms snap. Before the pain could catch up, the fists flashed again. The first blow caught his left biceps, turning muscle into mush. The force of the blow spun him halfway around. The other fist mashed muscle in his right arm. Suddenly his arms fell, helpless.

The vital spots were all open now.

Jishin was wearing the uniform for members of the company below management level. It was a tailored coverall in gray denim. On her feet she had jogging shoes. One of those joggers crushed the muscle along Uemurea's thigh.

He went crashing into the wall, only to rebound into a high kick that broke his sternum. He collapsed to the floor where more bone and muscle jellied under the impact of jogger heels.

When Jishin finally strode from the room, Uemurea was still partly conscious, drifting in and out of trauma shock. His body had no vital parts broken, but it would not survive the huge trauma to muscle and bone. The scientist's last coherent thought was that America was doomed.

July 2, 1023 hours, Fremont, California

RYAN VON STRADT could not keep a smug look of satisfaction off his face as fellow researcher, Doreen Morrison, prattled her jealous congratulations.

"I had no idea you were so close to a breakthrough, Ry. It's all so sudden."

"If you keep plugging, the details come together eventually," he assured her. But, he said it as though she had not been working hard.

She turned and strode down the hall, her heels beating an angry tune on the tile of the corridor. Von Stradt laughed as he unlocked the door to his electronics lab.

He locked the door behind him. He was not going to risk having someone barge in and find the source of his breakthrough thinking. He sat down at his personal computer.

Quickly he hooked up the telephone modem and instructed the computer to dial Small Chips.

He had received a brochure in the mail a week before. It had expounded the glories of a new data bank, designed especially for researchers in the electronics and computer field. The name, Small Chips, and the method of advertising had almost put him off trying it, but the introductory price was low, and Ryan von Stradt had been desperate—his computer research was going nowhere. So he had subscribed to Small Chips, and as soon as his access code arrived, he had scanned the contents of the bank with great eagerness.

At first he was disappointed in the size of the bank. Judging from the menu, it could not contain more than six or seven megabytes of information. But once he began scanning documents, he could not believe his eyes. All the information he needed to develop a new breed of computer was there. He took notes for several days and then announced that he had solved the problem of parallel chip connection. The stir the announcement caused made his ego soar.

Von Stradt was aware that Dr. Uemurea had been working on the same problem in Japan. Then terrorists had destroyed the research facility, razed it completely, and killed the staff. Von Stradt refused to ask himself why the information in Small Chips so closely paralleled Uemurea's research.

The Small Chips computer accepted his recognition code and he went immediately to the section he wanted and started making notes. Tomorrow he would start working on drawings and specs. Today he wanted to make sure that he gleaned all the information that would help him from Small Chips data bank. He became so engrossed in note taking, he did not even notice the first few shots.

When an automatic weapon went off in the hall outside the door, he looked up from the terminal. Then there was a frantic beating of fists on the door and Doreen Morrison's voice screaming to be let in. He quickly shut down the computer. He did not want her to guess the source of his inspiration on parallel chip connection.

He unlocked the door and opened it just in time to see his beautiful co-worker drop as bullets tore her body, spraying blood and bits of flesh all over the doorjamb. Ryan was a lot quicker at closing and relocking the door.

He ran to the telephone. The line was dead. It was time to evacuate. To hell with his breakthrough notes. He ran to the window. He was searching for something to use to break the sealed window when the locked door broke inward from a single blow that shattered the jamb. In the doorway stood a person—Von Stradt was not sure of the sex—a person that made his blood run cold. Long black hair was pulled into a ponytail that was doubled back on itself and bound with a rag. The face could have belonged to a prizefighter who had stayed in the ring a few too many years. The shoulders were broad and heavy. The body was covered by a gray mechanic's coverall, on the feet were joggers. The eyes were calm and deadly, the smile not at all warming.

"Thinking of going somewhere?" the person asked. The voice was flat, hoarse. It gave no clue to the sex of the speaker.

Von Stradt found no answer. He stood mutely while the thing glided in and turned on both his personal computer and his terminal to the company mainframe.

"Access codes?" it demanded.

"Uhhh," he stalled, wondering when someone was going to come and wake him from this nightmare.

"An old man down the hall tried to stall me and I poked an eye out," the hoarse voice said.

"Shit," he told the approaching demon.

Two knobby fists hit him on each side of the chest. Ryan fought to take a breath and his body exploded with pain. His knees buckled. He could not breathe, because each breath felt like he was cutting his chest with hot knives.

"Both lungs are pierced by broken ribs," the hoarse voice told him. "You'd better lie on your back and breathe with your diaphragm or you'll never last until help gets here."

He did as he was told. It helped some, but not much. "Get an ambulance," he croaked. Then he coughed and tasted the saltiness of blood.

"No access codes, no help," the voice told him.

Although it was agonizing to talk he mumbled the codes, first for the main computer and then for his personal computer.

After that, he was left alone while the strange being checked through the computer files. In a few minutes, it was through and shoved the terminals to the floor in anger.

"You're not a researcher," the hoarse voice spat. "There's not a single concept worth stealing. You're worthless."

The gray coveralls towered over him, filling his blurry vision. Then a foot came up and stomped down on his chest. The joggers and gray coveralls then left the room. They were the last thing that Ryan von Stradt saw as he choked to death on his own blood.

The police were investigating the crime two hours later when the bombs went off, leveling the Computer Development Company and killing all twelve of the police officers who were inside the building.

July 6, 1535 hours, Plainsfield, New Jersey

STANLEY KEEN III—known behind his back as Stan Three Sticks—looked down the boardroom table at the management team of Electronic Developments Inc. The general manager, marketing director, sales manager and comptroller all wore gray suits with a fine pinstripe, much like Stan's. The product-development manager, the only other member of the management team, wore the cheapest-looking denim suit that Keen had ever seen. The men all wore white shirts and plain, solid-colored ties, except the product director who wore an open-necked, solid green, uniform shirt. On his feet, which were propped up on the boardroom table, were cowboy boots.

"Are you idiots so bankrupt for ideas that you're going to start stealing them from the Japs?" the product-development manager asked.

"We are not stealing anything!" the comptroller shouted. "We paid the fee to use Small Chips. We're entitled to use all the information it contains."

"I'm all for that," the voice behind the cowboy boots drawled. "What I don't quite understand is why we want to pretend that we thought up the ideas in the first place. Everyone knows that old Uemurea did that work."

"You can't prove that's Uer...Ume...whoever's work," the sales manager said.

"So what? I can sure as hell prove it's not ours. We're not even working in the same area."

Before the four gray-suited managers burst blood vessels, Stan Three Sticks spoke up. "Let's address that question first. What is the advantage, if we claim we came up with the parallel process over giving credit where credit's due?"

"Patents, Mr. Keen. Patents," the general manager exclaimed. They were interrupted by screams and the sound of automatic fire outside the room.

Five gray suits turned toward the door. One pair of cowboy boots disappeared from the boardroom table and carried the owner in a long dive through a window. Five heads swiveled away from the door to look at the shattered window.

The door to the room was broken open and two figures wearing black hard hats peered into the room.

"Nothing but management," said one of the hard-hat wearers.

The other did not say a word. He tossed in a couple of fragmentation grenades and closed the door again. Five figures in gray suits watched fragmentation grenades roll across the room. They died watching.

An hour and ten minutes later, Miss Helen Argue showed the thirty-three pupils in her seventh-grade class into the reception area of Electronic Developments Inc. The students and the teacher were shocked to find that the reception area was decorated with three bullet-riddled bodies. Miss Argue hastily took her pupils back to the bus that had brought them. She had the driver keep them in the bus while she went back to telephone the police.

The police arrived in eight minutes. Miss Argue and four officers were killed when the building blew up. Eighteen pupils were injured, two blinded by flying glass.

Unfortunately for the free-spirited product-development manager, he returned to report to the police when he saw them arrive at the building.

2

July 7, 1948 hours, Atlanta, Georgia

Aya Jishin looked over the thirty long-noses crowded into the meeting room. She never thought she would get lonely for the sight of a civilized face, but she was. Nogi did not count. He was of Japanese origin, but too many brushes with Yakuza swords made him look more like an apple doll than a human. His appearance did not matter: he was willing to train barbarians to kill barbarians. That was all that counted.

"Good evening, former victims," she said, addressing the group. "You've been put out of work by automation. Now you're going to put the automators out of business."

The audience had to strain to catch her hoarse, croaked words, but they seemed to think it was worth the trouble. Shouts of assent greeted her opening remark.

She continued. "All of you joined Workers Against Redundancy because computers and automated machines have robbed you of your means of earning a living. WAR welcomed you, just as it's welcoming thousands of others each day. But the thirty of you were meant to do more than write to your congressmen, to be more effective than picketers, to pack more punch than a leaflet delivers. Welcome to the muscle and heart of WAR. You will form the local Harassment Initiation Team, known as HIT."

Being part of a hit team seemed to appeal to the audience. They cheered again.

Jishin waited for the cheering to stop. She expected it, not because she had any illusion that she was an orator, but because the unemployed long-noses had been carefully selected. She was speaking to the angriest of the angry, the ones who would take any excuse to strike out against the system.

She had already delivered the same speech in four other parts of the country, and there were still more HIT groups to start up. Wherever shortsighted government policies created large groups of unemployed, Jishin looked for a potential group of terrorists waiting for someone to come along and aim them at someone.

"We have had successful actions in both California and New Jersey," Jishin told her enthusiastic audience. "Tomorrow Georgia will know the real cost of using machines to rob people of their jobs and their self-respect."

While waiting for the cheering to again subside, Jishin smiled. There was plenty to smile about. These angry, homicidal long-noses represented only a small fraction of the unemployed. Others who were desperate for social action, but not willing to vent their hostilities in blood, were given jobs as volunteers for Workers Against Redundancy. WAR was the perfect front for selecting and training the psychotic misfits. As long as North American governments put such a low priority on full employment, she would never run out of cannon fodder.

Jishin walked over to a large-scale wall map and picked up a pointer. She instantly had the attention of the group.

"This is Elwood Industries. After tomorrow it will cease to exist."

She paused again, beginning to tire of all the cheering. She wanted to get to the meat of the briefing. That was the difficulty with using locals—too much energy had to be expended working on their enthusiasm. Her own squad of terrorists did not need all this. They knew that the real joy came from killing, torturing and maiming.

The cheering died down and they paid close attention. They knew that Nogi, the martial-arts instructor, would choose only half of them to join him and the seasoned veterans in the assault on Elwood Industries. That meant keen competition for the joys of battle and the even greater joys of combat pay.

Jishin quickly showed the audience her battle plan.

"So," she concluded, "tomorrow at three-thirty in the afternoon, those of you who qualify will get to write your names in the book of history as Americans who dared to stand up for mankind against the machine."

That was good for three minutes of cheering.

Jishin was glad it was over. She left the rostrum content. Six HIT units in place. No one could stop her now.

July 8, 1430 hours, over the Atlantic

SOMETHING POKED CARL LYONS in the ribs. He stayed relaxed as though he did not notice. The poke came again, stronger, more insistent.

Lyons's hand flew up in a blur of motion. His forearm connected with something hard that went flying. He tried to roll toward his attacker, but the seat belt restrained him.

Lyons opened his eyes. He was on the Stony Man executive jet. Pilot Jack Grimaldi and teammate Rosario Blancanales were standing over him. Lyons looked down the aisle of the Saberliner and saw Politician's stick lying on the carpeting.

Lyons flipped a lever and a small motor moved his seat to the upright position. He undid the lap belt and stretched before acknowledging the existence of the two men.

"Why'd you poke me with that stick?" Lyons demanded of Blancanales.

"Jack has a top-priority radio call waiting for you," Politician replied. He laughed. Waking Lyons was not as tough this time as it usually was.

"Who's flying this damn thing?" Lyons, still groggy, demanded.

"It's on autopilot," Grimaldi answered.

Lyons followed the pilot to the cockpit. He picked up the mike.

"Scrambler's on the broadcast," the pilot informed him.

Lyons settled into the copilot seat and pressed the transmit button.

"Ironman here."

Hal Brognola's voice sounded mechanical as it came out of the descrambler.

"Grimaldi still on line?"

"Yes. Shoot."

"What's your ETA southeastern seaboard?"

Lyons looked at Grimaldi who held up one clenched fist.

"About an hour," Lyons said.

"I'd like you to stop in Georgia and pick up a woman. We should talk to her, but my main worry is that terrorists will get to her first."

"So, send the federal marshals."

"If I read the situation correctly, the marshals would get wiped," Brognola insisted.

Lyons leaned back. "You'd better fill me in." He signaled to Grimaldi to set the course for Atlanta.

"There's been two computer-research facilities attacked by terrorists. Everyone has been butchered and the buildings bombed into rubble. In both cases the bombs were delayed to get the police when they started to investigate. We've been tracing down every possible link between the two places. The M.O. is the same, but one was in New Jersey and the other in California.

"Then a researcher—named Lao—in Atlanta reported that a new data bank contains the research notes of a Dr. Uemurea. We checked out Uemurea and found that he was killed and his lab destroyed much the same way as the two places that were destroyed here. After that we found that both places in the U.S. which were hit had just started to use the same data bank that Lao tells us has Uemurea's research in it.

"It's an outfit called Small Chips. I have a gut feeling that the research facility where Lao works will be next on the list. That's why I want Able Team there as quickly as possible. Those terrorists don't leave any survivors."

"Okay, Stony Man," Lyons said, ready to sign off.

"Hold it!" Brognola barked through the descrambler. "I've got a message coming in from Smyrna, near Atlanta. Stand by to receive."

"Standing by," Lyons told him.

Two minutes later, Brognola was back.

"How close an ETA can you give me, Ironman?"

Lyons glanced at Grimaldi who was operating the on-board computer.

Grimaldi took the mike from Lyons.

"Jack here, Hal. I can set us down at Hartfield in forty-one minutes at the present cruising speed, or I can burn the hell out of it and shave that to thirty-four minutes."

"Not good enough," Brognola said. "I just got word that people are collecting near Elwood Industries in Smyrna. The line went dead in the middle of the telephone conversation. I'm afraid it's going to go down any minute."

"Where is this place?" Grimaldi asked. As the coordinates and street address came in he fed the information to the flight computer. He then punched in a few numbers from his own head. While waiting for the few seconds it took the computer to respond, Grimaldi eased the throttle forward. The modified Rockwell T39 Saberliner screamed its delight and thrust Grimaldi and Lyons into the backs of their seats.

"I didn't think this can could peel air like this," Lyons said.

Grimaldi grinned. "Had the J603s replaced with a pair of J57-55s. They're both Pratt and Whitney's, but these afterburning turbos have more than twice the thrust. I've been looking for an excuse to see what this tour bus will do.

"You boys willing to hit silk?" Grimaldi asked.

"Lot safer than going joyriding with you," Lyons grunted back.

Grimaldi laughed and then spoke into the microphone. "Revised ETA for Elwood. I repeat, for Smyrna, not Hartfield, twenty-three minutes from now."

"Where are you landing?" Brognola demanded.

"I'm not landing, just dumping the freeloaders," Grimaldi replied.

"From a jet!"

"If you speak nice, I'll give them parachutes."

Brognola squawked but his faith in his men quickly overcame his skepticism. He knew they would need every second and every bit of concentration to do the job.

"Good luck," he said. "Signing off."

Already Lyons could detect a slight tremor in the plane. Grimaldi's casual manner was gone as he focused his full powers of concentration on keeping the quivering plane under control.

"Listen carefully," he told Lyons. "We have no time to go over this. I can't leave the controls or try to communicate again.

"I've been wanting to try this jump thing ever since I started flying this baby. You'll find chutes in the rear port locker. Get into them fast. When I cut all the power, get the door open. It opens inward. Be careful, it'll try to pull you out, even though I'll depressurize first.

"Then I'm going to pull the nose way up and this baby is going to stall. At that point, you'll be right over target. The three of you have eight seconds to get out before this baby tries backing up. Do it."

Lyons slapped Grimaldi on the shoulder.

"See you at the airport," he said. Then he made his way back to Pol and Gadgets.

"Scramble," he told them. "Gather up any ammunition and weapons you can carry. We jump in ten minutes."

Politician and Gadgets looked at each other. Lyons kept right on going and started pulling parachutes from the rear locker.

"He means it," Gadgets concluded.

He and Pol scrambled in their special flak jackets and started filling pockets with gun clips. Each warrior strapped on a web belt that held more gear. Lyons checked his Colt Python, which he holstered without its sound suppressor on his right hip. He slung the Atchisson Assault shotgun across his back before strapping on the parachute.

Politician grabbed the M-203, a combination M-16 and M-79 grenade launcher. He stored the grenades in a chest pouch. He looked and saw that Lyons had removed the sound suppressor from his Colt. Pol did the same thing with his 93-R before putting it in a breakaway rig on his left shoulder.

Gadgets had an Uzi clipped to his left leg and a 93-R under his left arm. He left the silencer on his weapon. He had radio gear strapped to his chest and a parachute on his back.

Lyons checked all the fastenings for Gadgets.

"What's coming down?" Politician asked. He was checking Lyons's chute to make sure it was on properly.

"Place called Elwood Electronics," Lyons answered. "Grimaldi's computer says come down in a vacant field a quarter mile away and head due west. It may be under terrorist attack by the time we get there. We've got to try and find some scientist named Lao. Brognola wants her delivered to Stony Man."

"How do we identify her?" Pol asked.

"Beats me," Lyons answered. He was inspecting Pol's harness by that time.

The engines wound down from a scream to silence. They immediately went to work on the door, pulling it in and sliding it back.

"Remember," Lyons shouted over the noise, "all of us out in eight seconds. Pol first, Gadgets, then me."

Just then the plane nosed upward and lost speed. The three fighters had to hang on to bulkheads and seats to keep from being shoved to the rear, past the opening.

Lyons slapped Politician on the shoulder. Pol already holding on to both sides of the doorway. One hard pull and he was gone. Gadgets placed both hands on the tail side of the opening and peeled himself through. He was barely clear of the opening when Lyons pushed off from a seat with both feet and dived through the door after him. Lyons pulled his rip cord almost immediately. He knew the other two would delay for several seconds, using the variation in timing to spread themselves out.

As his shroud lines began to play out, Lyons glanced at the plane. It was motionless above him, almost standing on its tail. Then suddenly it slipped to one side and twisted, falling like a broken toy. Soon it was well below the jumpers. As the wind speed increased, the nose began to lead the rest of the plane. Then the two huge tail jets flamed in and the machine was in a power dive. From above it looked as though the mad air jockey had managed to pull the black bird out of its dive with only a few hundred feet to spare.

3

July 8, 1530 hours, Smyrna, Georgia

The attack on Elwood Industries went off like the well-planned military campaign that it was. The only thing that separated it from actual war was the fact that heavily armed, well-trained thugs were going up against unarmed civilians.

At precisely 1530, three trucks stopped on the three access roads to Elwood Industries and set up roadblocks. Men in coveralls halted traffic and told drivers there would be a half-hour delay while a crew located a large gas leak.

At 1532, a man and a woman in a stolen telephone-company truck went down an access hatch and cut the lines to Elwood Industries and all the neighboring plants. When an off-duty security guard stopped to pass the time of day, the man and woman took turns practicing their karate blows. Then they stuffed the body into the access space and replaced the hatch cover.

The Elwood building was surrounded precisely on schedule, at 1540. Two minutes later, three teams of four men each went into the building by its three different entrances.

At the front entrance, the receptionist's smile died when she saw the two M-16s and the double-barreled shotgun carried by the three terrorists who followed Aya Jishin. Jishin's hands were empty, but that did not make her look any less menacing than the others.

"Where do I find Lao?" Jishin demanded.

The receptionist turned white.

Jishin grabbed her arm, held it over the edge of the desk and broke it with a single blow.

"Where?" Jishin asked.

"The end of corridor three on the right," the receptionist screamed.

"That's better," Jishin said and strode out of the reception area, leaving her henchmen to kill the receptionist.

The one with the shotgun blasted her face into gory bits.

Jishin found corridor three and marched grimly to the end. Gunshots sounded elsewhere in the building. Doors in corridor three began to open and heads poked out of doorways.

"Get back in your offices," Jishin shouted.

A fat balding man stepped out in front of the striding terrorist.

"What's this all about?" he demanded.

"Just do as you're told," Jishin ordered.

The man did not move.

"I demand an immediate answer."

Jishin had been forced to come to a halt by the fat form blocking her way.

"What do you do here that you can demand anything?" Jishin countered in her hoarse voice.

The man grinned in the knowledge of his own power. "I'm the vice-president and the comptroller here. And who do you think you are?"

"Then you aren't a researcher?"

"You seem slow to get the message."

"Then we don't need you," Jishin told him. Her fists blurred and the fat man screamed.

For a moment the only sound that could be heard in the corridor was the whack, whack, whack of fists smashing meat. The vice-president and comptroller slid down the wall, leaving a streak of red. He died in a large heap on the floor.

Doors slammed. Jishin was alone in the corridor, except for the three terrorists who had followed her into the reception room.

"Go down this hall," she told them. "If the person is a researcher, leave him for me, if not kill him. Move."

They moved, grinning in anticipation of more targets for their weapons.

Shots sounded from another portion of the building.

"George," Jishin commanded, "tell those trigger-happy slobs to wait until you've sorted them before they start shooting people who don't resist."

George lowered his shotgun and went to obey orders. He was clearly irked that he had to put aside his work to straighten out the amateurs.

"Don't you two start without me," he barked at his fellow jackals.

The door at the end of corridor three was locked. Jishin used a front kick to smash the catch. The door swung back with so much force that the knob smashed the plaster wall. A diminutive Oriental woman looked up from one of the electronics workbenches. She seemed more curious than startled. Jishin tried to place the country of origin, but could not. The small woman looked Vietnamese.

"Where's Dr. Lao?" the terrorist leader demanded.

Although the small face retained its Oriental calm, Jishin detected a flicker of amusement in the eyes. The hands continued to solder small parts.

"Dr. Lao's busy and doesn't wish to be disturbed," the woman said. Much to Jishin's surprise, the English had the accenting given by Japanese.

Jishin had her concentration broken by a heavy dose of firing somewhere in the building. If those long-noses did not learn discipline soon, she would kill them herself. A deep boom derailed her train of thought. She knew that nothing her forces carried spoke with such authority.

She reached into a coverall pocket, pulled out a compact communicator and hit the red broadcast button.

"Is the perimeter patrol on channel?" she asked.

"Perimeter patrol leader here," the small unit answered almost immediately.

"We're under attack. Move the perimeter force in for backup," Jishin ordered.

"Move in, roger."

She did not bother acknowledging, but put the communicator back into her coveralls.

"Roger," she snorted to herself. *"Baka!"*

The small woman overheard the muttered "fool!" and laughed. "It must be terrible to attract such incompetent people to serve such a worthy mistress," she sympathized. Her Japanese was so heavily inferior addressing superior that it was insulting.

A mere technician would never have thought to use language in that sarcastic fashion.

"*You* are Dr. Lao," Jishin stated.

"So I am," the woman agreed.

Jishin strode to the computer terminal in one corner of the lab.

"What is your access code?" she demanded.

"None of your business," Dr. Lao told her in a quiet, calm voice that was still faintly tinged with amusement.

Jishin sighed. "I suppose I must do some persuading."

She walked around the edge of the workbench and approached Lao. Lao slid off the stool she was using and stood waiting. She seemed expectant, not alarmed.

Jishin noticed the relaxed stance, the careful placement of the feet. She knew she was meeting a martial artist, but was uncertain of the art practiced. The style hardly mattered. Someone that frail was not going to be able to block a *shotokan* karate blow.

Jishin launched a feint at Lao's head, followed by a fist to the chest. It was nothing fancy, but it would serve to demonstrate that nothing could stop a well-launched blow.

The chest was not there. The fist went by the slim woman. There was a tug on Jishin's sleeve, her forward momentum increased and she stumbled into a wall. She straightened up and shook her head. Now she knew the fighting style. This small twerp was about to die because she trusted aikido. Useless bunk, it meant standing around and waiting for the other person to attack.

Jishin executed a roundhouse kick, followed by a snap punch toward the face, followed by a knee lift to the groin. She had never seen aikido effectively used against a determined triple attack. The roundhouse kick received the nudge that Jishin knew it would. She was braced to counter it. She used her counterforce to launch the blow toward the face. The small aikido fighter spun away from the blow, receiving the knee lift to the rump instead of the groin. She stumbled into the wall.

Jishin laughed and kicked the small rear end, sending her opponent slamming harder into the wall. Lao hit the plaster with a loud slapping sound, but instead of bouncing back into Jishin's waiting hands, she spun away along the wall. Lao stopped about ten feet away, obviously dizzy and confused.

Jishin closed in rapidly, noting with satisfaction the cut over the scientist's right eye. The terrorist promised herself that before she was through, she would use that cut to peel away the entire damned face. Jishin felt great; it was a relief to find someone who could put up even a bit of a fight.

Jishin's punch was thrown too rapidly. Another tug at her sleeve and she spun from her own momentum. Suddenly Jishin's back was to her opponent, who quickly planted a small foot on her rump and shoved the terrorist into the wall so hard she broke plaster with her face.

Jishin bounced off the wall straight at the small scientist. The terrorist's fist shot out but it never connected; Lao deflected it up and outward, using the force picked up from her attacker to spin and plant a small fist in Jishin's armpit. The shot would have rendered most fighters unconscious, but it merely made Jishin stagger back and plant her feet firmly, ready to be rushed, but waiting for her head to clear.

Lao did not make the mistake of rushing an experienced fighter simply because she was groggy. The aikido fighter waited, calm, composed, just out of reach. There was no attempt to escape or call for help. For the first time Jishin wondered if she could beat the diminutive woman who stood, eyeing her curiously.

There was more gunfire, but Jishin forced herself to concentrate on the job at hand. She had a killing to perform. There was no way she would allow her troops to discover that such a small person had even slowed her down. Jishin erupted with a savage yell and a high kick at Lao's chest.

The kick was deflected with a small hard fist to the calf. Jishin found her leg painful to stand on. Even more painful was the way the small woman stood, patiently waiting to see what would happen next.

The door to the lab was splintered off the frame, falling flat on the floor. Nogi entered, closely followed by two of the experienced terrorists.

"Shoot her," Jishin told her followers.

As SOON AS they hit the ground, the members of Able Team cut parachute harnesses and let the breeze play with the empty chutes. They took off toward the building from which emerged screams and the sound of gunfire.

Two of the perimeter guards had moved in to investigate the parachutes. There was no mistaking the fit figures in olive drabs from the terrorists in coveralls. The two terrorists stopped and steadied their M-16s on target.

Gadgets checked over his shoulder and saw the two dropping into firing position. He shouted the one word that he knew would bring instant reaction from his companions.

"Ambush!"

Instantly, the three running warriors dived for the ground. Hastily fired .223 tumblers swarmed over their heads, humming their sound of angry destruction. Gadgets did a shoulder roll to the left, coming back to his feet in a crouch, facing the enemy. Lyons and Pol landed in opposite ditches, eyes peeled for other terrorists.

Gadgets's Uzi, without the folding shoulder stock, easily yanked free of the clip on his left thigh. He worked the first bullet into the chamber and acquired the target. Before the would-be assassins could readjust their aims to allow for the sudden scattering of their targets, a figure eight of 9mm manglers had blown them both backward onto the road. Able Team was on its way again before terrorist boot heels stopped scraping the pavement.

The three warriors took the front door into the reception

area. One look at the minced body of the receptionist told them they were already late.

"I hope we can still save some of them," Pol rumbled.

They ran through the reception area without slowing, turning left to find themselves in a large, open office area. Four men and a woman in coveralls, held captive an office force of eleven. Lyons broke right, seeking an angle of fire. Pol and Gadgets dropped flat in the doorway. Gadgets's Uzi spoke first, a three-round burst that took the legs out from under the terrorist closest to the captives. The stutter of the Uzi grabbed attention away from Lyons. Automatic rifles stopped zeroing in on the large blond man and swung back toward the doorway.

Politician's M-203 spoke next. A single, carefully aimed shot entered a terrorist's left eye and blossomed in a small fountain of gore from the crown of the head.

Terrorist bullets, fired in panic, began chopping up the doorway. That won Lyons time to flank the terrorists. He stood where they formed a row of targets, with the captives on one side and the doorway holding Pol and Gadgets on the other. The Atchisson Assault 12 shotgun spoke twice with booming authority.

The two goons closest to Lyons disintegrated from the waist up. They became a barrage of chunky red debris. The one farthest from Lyons remained recognizable as a human being, but she was just as dead.

"Dr. Lao, where is she?" Lyons barked at the terrified staff.

His commanding voice rallied several workers from their state of shock and bewilderment. Three hands pointed back past the reception area. "She's in the end office, third hallway."

"Thanks. Now, get out of here," Pol commanded. He pointed to a fire exit at the end of the room.

Pol and Gadgets then followed Lyons who was already on his way toward the other side of the building.

The first corridor they encountered had a single terrorist guard at one end. She lounged against the wall at the mouth of the hall, her 16-gauge shotgun pointing down the passageway, keeping victims confined to their offices until they could be questioned. At that moment it was the wrong way for the shotgun to be pointing.

Gadgets sent three bullets through the terrorist's brain. She died before she realized she was in trouble.

A half-gagged shout of pain came from the next hallway. Able Team rounded the corner on the run. Three terrorists were questioning a prisoner. Two had M-16s slung over their shoulders and were holding the arms of a man in a white coat. A third had the tip of a pump action, 12-gauge Marlin Glenfield pointed at the man's face. A trickle of blood ran down the victim's chin from where the muzzle had knocked out a tooth. The lab worker's knees had buckled and much of his weight was being supported by the two who were holding his arms.

"Tell us again what you do here," the holder of the shotgun was demanding.

The three terrorists were having so much fun, they did not hear the other armed force until Able Team was on them. Lyons thrust the warm barrel of the Atchisson under the questioner's chin.

The two who were holding the victim let go and tried to swing the M-16s from their shoulders. It was a futile effort. Pol smashed his M-203 into the temple of one, killing him instantly as fragments of skull lacerated animal brain. Gadgets crushed the other's windpipe with his fist, leaving the goon to roll on the floor, choking on his own tissue and blood.

Lyons's shotgun was thrust under the chin so hard that the man was stretched to the tips of his toes. He tried bringing his shotgun around to bear on Lyons.

"Don't lose your head," Lyons told him.

The goon's shotgun continued to swing. Lyons's finger tightened on the trigger. He decorated the corridor with atomized head.

"Move," Lyons instructed the saved man in the white coat. He ran for cover.

A cluster of whizzes sent Able Team diving for safety inside one of the offices.

"Reinforcements," Lyons guessed. "You two find Lao. I'll keep the lice off your asses."

"Cover me," Gadgets told him.

Lyons threw himself on his stomach and squirmed out the door. Before the hail of lead could drop to his level, he sent two blasts from the Atchisson back up the hall. He was rewarded with a chorus of screams from dying terrorists.

While Lyons fired Gadgets dashed across the hall and booted open the opposite office door. He glanced inside to make sure it was empty and then retreated back to the office where his teammates waited. Politician had an HE grenade with an impact detonator loaded into the launcher. As soon as Gadgets was out of the line of fire, he fired the grenade into the far wall of the opposite office.

Lyons sent two more discouraging messages up the hallway while both Gadgets and Pol crossed the corridor.

Two quick kicks enlarged the hole in the opposite wall and made it easy to climb through. Pol and Gadgets found themselves in a lab on the third corridor.

The two warriors ran for the door.

Gadgets tossed a fragmentation grenade up the third corridor to discourage two terrorists. As soon as the blast came, he and Pol raced the other way to the last doorway in the hall. There was no door left to worry about.

Pol jumped into the room, crouched, ready for action.

By the time Gadgets was through the doorway, terrorists were pouring lead down the hallway after him. The Uzi sent half a clip back up the hall. Those terrorists who were able retreated to the shelter of the cross corridor.

WHEN JISHIN TOLD the terrorists to shoot Lao, the computer expert sized up the three additional menaces that had entered her lab. The one in the lead had a seamed face that had met too many blades. He carried an ugly submachine gun, a Japanese-made SCK model 65. The other two had

Army-surplus M-16s. She knew she must act quickly or be shot.

The hands wrapped around the SCK were callused from karate. That gave Lao her inspiration. She spoke quickly in Japanese before the terrorists could obey the command.

"This frail old lady needs bullets to help her. I had just kicked her ass when you interrupted."

The plaster on Jishin's face was incontrovertible proof of Lao's words. Two men quickly turned to hide their grins. The cut-up one did not bother. He laughed out loud. Jishin's eyes narrowed with humiliation and fury.

"Maybe women are too soft to become true *karateka*," the scarred one muttered.

Jishin's voice was like ice. "Perhaps our worthy karate *sensei* would condescend to demonstrate to this student?"

Nogi sobered immediately. He had gone too far and his leader would not forgive this loss of face. But Nogi's own dignity would not let him back down at that point. He handed his weapon to Jishin.

"I will try, though if she has given you difficulties, I will need the blessings of the gods to preserve my own skin," he said.

Jishin laughed at him, confirming the knowledge that there would be no forgiveness from her. He knew she would not kill him as long as she needed him to train these stupid, long-nosed recruits, but the knowledge brought him no comfort at all.

Nogi, karate instructor and trainer of killers, advanced almost casually on his prey. He looked as if he was still getting ready to fight when his foot flashed out like a bolt of lightning. The kick was intended to make a field goal with Lao's head.

Lao bent away from the kick and her small hands grabbed the extended ankle. Then she moved in a large circle. Her left foot described a graceful arc ending in Nogi's exposed crotch.

Jishin decided that losing the karate instructor was a small price to pay for getting Lao out of the way. She brought up the SCK, but pride prevented her from pulling the trigger. She had to regain face by pulverizing that little woman.

In the moment that Jishin hesitated, the decision slipped through her fingers.

Two men in combat fatigues burst through the doorway. One turned back to cover their tails while the other faced the room, bringing his automatic weapon to bear on the two startled terrorists with the M-16s. Jishin felt a momentary pang of envy that someone opposing her should be able to command such fine warriors.

Jishin had the SCK in firing position. She was already targeted on the intruder.

As Jishin squeezed the trigger to cut up the interlopers with 9mm parabellums, she was jolted forward, causing the deadly blast to chew up flooring. The wooden stool, which Lao had been sitting on when Jishin broke into the lab, bounced off her back and clattered around her feet.

The two terrorists with the M-16s brought them up with well-trained precision. Well-trained precision was too slow. Blancanales already had a figure eight of .223 tumblers chewing into them and throwing them onto their backs. Dying fingers sent sporadic bursts into the ceiling.

Gadgets's Uzi sent another batch of death chattering up the hallway, teaching caution to the terrorist reinforcement.

Throwing the stool had taken Lao's attention off Nogi. In spite of the pain he was suffering, he got off the floor and hit her with a quick ax-hand across the upper vertabrae. It was not sufficient to kill the small woman, but it rendered her almost unconscious. Nogi held her for a shield against Politician's firepower.

When Jishin recovered her balance, she snatched up the stool and heaved it backward through the lab's window.

Pol noticed her maneuvers peripherally, but he was also absorbing the drama between Nogi and Lao. The problem of getting the small research scientist away from the two *karateka* was not an easy one. He decided to eliminate the terrorist in the open first. As he brought the M-203 to bear on Jishin, she dropped the empty SCK and made a headfirst dive out the window. He swung the weapon back on the male.

The man was a wily fighter. Although he was larger than his semiconscious victim, he kept dodging and weaving behind her, never offering a clear target for as much as a half second. As he did so, he edged toward the broken window.

Politician let go of his weapon and made his own head-first dive across a laboratory table. Nogi had the choice of abandoning his hostage, or finding himself in a melee with an aikido expert and a warrior of unknown abilities.

Nogi shoved his hostage into Politician's flight path, and joined his leader in trying to earn his wings from a first-floor window.

Politician could not change the course of his headfirst dive. He could only sweep Lao to him and roll so that he landed on his back with the woman on top of him. She was small, but she was an incredibly compact bundle of human being. The impact knocked the wind out of Politician.

Lao had been surprised to see the savvy, white-haired warrior react with such total disregard for his own safety. She lay sprawled on top of Politician, collecting her wits.

Gadgets fired his Uzi.

"They're pushing a steel bench up the hall ahead of them," he called to Pol.

As POLITICIAN AND GADGETS vanished along their newly created cross corridor, Lyons waited until a terrorist looked around the corner and then opened the goon's head with a choice selection of double-ought and number-two lead balls. With the terrorists at the head of the hall taken care of, Lyons walked to the back wall of the office and put his fist through it.

It took only seconds to punch and kick an opening through the plasterboard into the adjacent office. Two karate front kicks took one of the two-by-four studs out of his way. He stepped through and opened a door to the first corridor.

The corridor served the rarified and protected areas where the company computer worked. Several technicians were being forced at gunpoint to make the computer disgorge information for the benefit of terrorists who would rather destroy than build.

Lyons's right hand went to his hip and came back filled with Colt Python. He stood in the doorway to the computer room and let the Python sting each head whose body held a gun. Four terrorists had their tapes erased in three seconds. Only the last reacted swiftly enough to get a shot off—it went harmlessly into the ceiling.

The bewildered technicians stood motionless, staring at head-smashed terrorists. Lyons stood looking at the ceiling, where the blast from the dying terrorist's gun had removed an acoustic tile. There was a four-foot crawl space above the tiles. Before the computer technicians could recover their wits, the large blond man who had just exterminated their captors leaped onto a high-speed tape-drive cabinet. From there he pushed a couple of sound tiles out of the way and disappeared into the ceiling. He said nothing to them.

When Lyons reached an end wall, he carefully removed a ceiling tile and looked down. He was over the cross corridor. Twenty feet along, four terrorists were peering down the second hallway.

Lyons pulled a frag from his web belt, held it to the count of three and tossed it into the midst of the four.

"What's. . ." began one man as the grenade fell past his eyes. That was as far as any of them got.

Lyons leaped from the crawl space and advanced toward the third corridor, Atchisson in debating position.

WHEN GADGETS ANNOUNCED that the terrorists were coming up the hall behind a shield, Lao rolled off Pol and the Able Team warrior leaped to his feet.

Lao Ti had given herself up for dead the moment Jishin had broken into the laboratory. As all effective warriors must do, she considered each second of life a postponement of the inevitable. Now these two strange fighters had bought her an entirely new existence. Suddenly life seemed to sparkle as it never had before. Although for twenty-eight of her thirty-two years she had been trained in the warriors' way, never before had her life been so close to being over. The *new* life was a gloriously bright and profound thing. She savored it deeply.

Blancanales was too preoccupied with the sounds of gunfire and the advancing enemy to really appreciate the situation, but he was very aware of what was happening in Lao's mind. It was an experience he had felt after many close encounters with death, but it was a feeling that was impossible to share.

As Pol dashed to retrieve the M-203, he introduced himself and Gadgets.

Politician snatched up the M-203 and shoved a frag into the launcher as he ran for the doorway. He peered out at the steel bench, slowly advancing the length of the hall. It was less than twenty feet from the broken door to the lab.

Pol aimed carefully and shot the grenade over the top of the bench. It went too far and did only minor damage to the terrorists.

"Get ready to crouch and run," Pol told Gadgets.

Politician plucked an HE with a contact detonator from his bandolier. He shot the charge straight into the side of the steel table. Pol, Gadgets and Lao ducked, opened their mouths and covered their ears against the shock wave that bounced back down the hall. As soon as the shock wave hit them, they were up and running down the hall toward the steel workbench.

Gadgets, who was in the lead, suddenly yelled.

"Hit dirt!"

The three of them dropped as the recognizable booming of the Atchisson Assault 12 filled the air with noise and a hail of death. When the booming stopped, Gadgets and Pol shouted and then popped over the top of the steel barrier, ready to finish off any surviving terrorists. There were none.

In the silence after the shooting, they could hear the sound of a siren outside.

Lao, Gadgets and Politician joined Lyons in the cross corridor.

Lyons dug an ID wallet out of a pocket.

"Let's go see if this damn thing works," Lyons said.

Officer Jim Gillies of the Atlanta Police Department was the first on the scene of a reported gun battle. He had just stopped his cruiser in front of Elwood Electronic Industries when four people emerged from the front door. Three wore combat fatigues; a small, Oriental female wore a white smock. The men carried the meanest collection of automatic weapons that the young officer had ever seen.

He later tried to tell his fellow officers about the experience: "One was a fully-automatic 12-gauge, honest to God. I decided not to bother drawing the .32 the department gives us. Those weapons made me feel like I was carrying a peashooter. I sort of wanted to hide it. You know what I mean?"

He paused, but none of his brother officers told him that they knew what he meant.

"Well, before I could get out, they all got into my squad car. In the front seat, right beside me, was the meanest looking dude I've ever seen. With eyes like those, I don't see why he figured he needed those guns he was carting around.

"He flashed a Justice Department buzzer at me and said, 'The airport.'"

His fellow officers were hooked.

"What the hell did you do?" one demanded.

"I drove them to the bloody airport. What the hell do you think I did?" Gillies replied.

"Those credentials could have been faked," someone pointed out.

Gillies sighed. "You didn't see those men. You didn't see those eyes beside me, and you didn't see those weapons. That buzzer could have been from the Pretoria Department of Sanitation, I would have still driven them to the damn airport.

"The airport security didn't argue either. We picked up a pilot at the gate and went straight to a black jet marked Acme Pest Control, honest to God."

"It was nice working with you," one of the other officers said.

Gillies shrugged. He was not going to try to explain that someone from Washington had already straightened the mess out.

4

July 9, 1420 hours, Stony Man Farm, Virginia

Lao Ti gave a roll of solder back to Gadgets.

"Not acid core, resin core," she instructed.

Gadgets pulled a two-pound roll of the desired solder from a drawer in the workbench.

Hal Brognola, the head Fed at Stony Man, sat on a high wooden bar stool, looking uncomfortable and a bit irritated.

"Why do we have to hold a briefing in Gadgets's workshop?" he asked.

Ti had a Kaypro 10 scattered across one of the workbenches and was in the midst of adding two extra boards that she had made up herself. She answered without looking up.

"So I can finish this computer. Please go ahead. I will listen most attentively."

Aaron Kurtzman, Stony Man's erstwhile top computer man who was paralyzed from the waist down by a bullet taken in the bloody Stony Man smash, swung around in his wheelchair. "That was a good computer before you took it apart."

"A toy," she replied. "The RAM was only 64K, and the reaction time abominable."

"Some people consider that toy the best portable computer on the market," Kurtzman, "The Bear," reminded the computer scientist. Kurtzman's knowledge of computers was enormous. But now, because of injuries, his job status was that of computer-maintenance man.

She nodded in agreement.

"I'm remodeling it to suit our needs. I've kept the case,

the hard disk drive, and the floppy drive. I yanked the microprocessor and the minute memory chips. Mr. Brognola found me some of the new, compact, geranium arsenide chips at NASA. I put those in with parallel microprocessors. Of course, that meant too much heat. So Gadgets helped me install this small, high-velocity fan at the back and improve the cooling ducts. Then I changed the addressing system on the hard disk. So now this little computer is faster, and stronger.

"Now I'm building in a compact telephone modem. Clear?"

Kurtzman's eyes sparkled. He was impressed. "Very," he said. "What will the computer do now?"

Ti finished soldering a crowded connection before answering. "It has about half the response time it had before. Instead of 64K of random access memory, it has a megabyte. The disk now stores fifteen megabytes quite reliably."

Kurtzman whistled. "That's a lot of computer."

"You asked what it will do. I'll tell you, because this is your specialty. I'm putting together a program. I'll need Stony Man's help and all the computer space you can steal. We want this little computer to be able to talk to strangers.

"It will not be easy, but it is possible. We hook this to a strange computer. First, it must analyze the microprocessor and the strange computer's addressing system. Then it listens to the computer for a while and decides which programming language has been used. Once it tells us all that, we can talk to the strange computer, have it tell us what it knows, and even tell it what to do."

The Bear shook his head. "Anyone who could do that, could end up owning every dollar in America."

Lao grinned. "That's a thought. We'd better not publish our program. But because these terrorists are using computers and data banks to go after us, I thought it might be helpful if we could use their own computers to go after them."

Ti turned her attention to Brognola. "You were going to brief us?"

Brognola dug right in to the topic.

"First," he said, "the bodies at Elwood Electronics. No identification. The coverall uniform doesn't help. They're the largest-selling national brand. Several of the dead terrorists had records, several are known internationally. On two bodies we found membership cards that link them to WAR."

"Which war?" Ti asked.

"That's W-A-R, Worker's Against Redundancy. It's a union of the unemployed that lays all the blame for high unemployment on automation and computers," Brognola replied.

"That makes some sort of connection," Politician mused.

Brognola continued. "We've done some research on WAR. The organization is nationwide and has regional offices in Boston, Atlanta, Houston, Minneapolis, Salt Lake City and San Francisco. At each of those offices there seems to be a core group. They call the core groups Harassment Initiation Teams."

"You're putting us on. No one would be that blatant," Gadgets protested.

"I'm not putting anyone one. Those initials are H-I-T, hit. We don't seem to be able to get a handle on what HIT is supposed to do, but we're beginning to have our suspicions."

"What's the plan?" Lyons interrupted.

Brognola fastened his eyes on Lyons. "We need more intelligence before we can go ahead," he said. "We should try to get someone inside one of those Harassment Initiation Teams, and we should try to get a tap on their computer. We've traced back Small Chips on the computer net, and we're reasonably sure that it comes from WAR's main computer in California."

"That's why I'm putting this thing together," Ti added.

"How long will it take to crack their computer?" Lyons asked.

Lao thought before answering. "Hard to tell. I'll finish this today. I could leave for California tonight. I want to find an office close to theirs. Then it all depends how long it will take to penetrate their security.''

"Take Gadgets and Pol," Lyons said. "They'll get you inside overnight. That means I'm going to have to get inside a Harassment Initiation Team in a hell of a hurry.''

"Hold on," Brognola shouted.

"Two of those terrorists got away. They can identify you.''

Lyons shook his head. "They can identify Pol and Gadgets. None of the scum who saw me are able to tell anyone about it.

"I think I'll go back to Atlanta to join. Maybe I'll get lucky and meet that witch woman and her Japanese sidekick. Besides, they're short of troops there. They should be hiring.''

Brognola opened his mouth and then closed it again. "You want this?''

Lyons nodded.

"Okay. We'll play it that way. We still need a trap to bait. I was thinking that I would set up shop in Atlanta. We can probably get Elwood Electronic Industries running again. Then, when we're ready to set bait for our terrorists, we'll have a base.''

Lyons nodded his approval of the idea.

Brognola looked at his shoes for a moment.

"What else is on your mind?" Politician prompted.

Brognola looked up, some internal decision made.

"I took what evidence I have to the President," he said. "It's an election year. He will do absolutely nothing that makes it look as if he is investigating or in any way harassing the unemployed. We're on our own on this. No cooperation from other departments. No acknowledgment from the President that he even knows we exist. We can't even check in with the local police forces.''

Lyons got up and started for the door. Over his shoulder he snorted. "So what. Let's get to work.''

5

July 10, 1950 hours, Atlanta, Georgia

The night was still early by the standards of the Southern Hospitality Bar—most of the regulars not arriving until after eight, but already the stools along the bar were filled. Georgios Zosimas looked down at a bigmouth on the end. The Greek-born barkeep had a ten-percent interest in the Southern Hospitality, and a definite interest in keeping the place friendly.

However, there had been a lot like the bigmouth in the bar lately. They had one thing in common: they mouthed off about the way society was screwing the working man. The big guy with the blond hair was no exception. At least now Georgios knew what to do about the yappy bastard.

As Georgios approached that end of the bar, the guy on the stool next to the mouthpiece spoke up. "If you don't like this country, you can always go back to where you came from."

"I'm there," the big guy growled. "Now, why the hell don't you go back to Shitsville where you come from? Your sister hasn't been able to find anyone to lay her since you left."

Georgios hurried the last few steps, anxious to prevent mayhem.

"We don't allow talk like that in here," he said to the blond.

Georgios Zosimas transferred his attention to the guy who had been insulted. His mouth suddenly went dry. He did not know the man's name, but knew him as one tough customer. He had once broken the arm of a customer who had accidentally slopped beer on him. If these two big guys started slugging it out, they could wreck the place.

"Let's step outside," the insulted man said.

"Piss off," the blond spat. He caught the other's flying fist in his right hand. He held it and began to squeeze. The owner of the fist slowly changed color from fury red to agony white. He brought his other hand into action and tried to pry the hand from his fist. The hand convulsed tighter. A bone cracked.

"You're leaving to have your broken hand set, aren't you?" the mouthy man said.

Sweat had broken out on the other man's face, in spite of the air-conditioning.

"Yeah," he grated.

"Yeah, what?"

"Yeah, I'm leaving now to get my hand set," the man said through the pain.

"You still haven't got it right, mister. Try again. Yeah, what?" the mouthy bastard with the icy eyes repeated.

"Yes, sir."

"That's better."

Georgios did not wait to see any more; he hurried to the telephone.

Lyons watched the barkeep make his hurried call. He hoped that it would produce a small Japanese with deformed hands and a face like a road map.

Lyons was not much for role playing, but he could do it if he had to. His way of playing the present role was simple—he just acted like a person the real Carl Lyons could not resist pounding.

The problem was that he could not stand himself. The longer he had to live with the creep he had created, the more he wanted to throw up.

This was only the second bar Lyons had tried. He was systematically choosing the drinking spots that were closest to the building where Workers Against Redundancy had their offices. Sooner or later, he expected to meet someone from HIT, someone who would recognize a kindred spirit. He hoped it was sooner rather than later, because Lyons felt he was in danger of punching himself out.

A few minutes later, he knew he had hit pay dirt. A Japanese slipped onto the stool beside him. Only one Japanese in North America could have the hacked-up face and the knobby fists that Politician had described.

"Did you stock some sake?" the newcomer asked the barman.

"Yes, Mr. Nogi. This bottle's on the house."

The barkeep produced a small bottle of clear fluid and worked the cork free.

"Please heat it," he was told.

Lyons nursed his beer in sullen silence, listening to the interchange, but not looking at the man on the adjacent stool. He had mouthed off enough to attract the fish. Now he must play hard to get.

When the barkeep brought back the heated bottle and a shot glass, the Japanese nodded briefly at Lyons and raised an eyebrow. Georgios nodded to signify that the large blond was the man he had telephoned about. The Japanese, looking almost presentable in a gray suit, shook his head slightly to signify that this was not a man for whom he was responsible. Georgios's face fell.

"I'm sorry, Mr. Nogi. He sure sounds like the others. He's not at all happy about being out of work."

"Very few people are, Mr. Zosimas. Thank you for calling me, but this is not one of my trainees."

The Japanese paused and then continued. "However, if he's making difficulties, I'll be glad to persuade him to leave when I leave."

The bartender glanced doubtfully from the small Japanese to the large, mean-looking customer beside him.

Nogi smiled. "I guarantee there will be no fuss and no damage."

There was something about that smile that made Georgios even more nervous than before. He struggled to keep his fears off his face.

"Thank you, Mr. Nogi."

The Japanese nodded, his face was blank. His mind was full of contempt for stupid Westerners who could not conceal the most elementary of feelings. It was time to demonstrate how easy it all was. The friendship of the barkeep helped keep the trainees in line. So Nogi would make a duly impressive demonstration. Nogi sighed when he thought of all the trainees he had lost. Having to start over again with another batch of stinking long-noses was a repulsive future to contemplate. He would certainly like to get his hands on the Americans who had ruined the raid on Elwood Electronic Industries.

He sipped his sake. He wished the stupid American would mouth off again. It would make everything much easier.

Lyons signaled for another beer. When Georgios brought it, he grabbed the barkeep's hand.

"Were you talking about me to that gook?" he demanded.

Georgios looked at those icy blue eyes and then looked away. Nogi saw genuine fear there. He inserted himself into the conversation.

"Mr. Zosimas made it a point to let me know that you are out of work. I work for an organization that helps the unemployed."

The blue eyes looked into his. They reflected suspicion.

"My business is *my* business," the man said.

"I may have a job for you."

"Fat chance."

Nogi was beginning to hope he could recruit this one. A good instructor always throws the largest member of the class around when doing demonstrations. Nogi would enjoy throwing this one around.

Nogi took another drink of hot sake. "I could teach someone your size to be really effective in combat. You'd be paid for learning."

"You recruiting for the army?"

"I'm recruiting people to fight the injustices that leave good men without jobs." Nogi said it mechanically.

Lyons drank half his beer nonstop, then slammed his glass down. "Sounds like bullshit," he spat.

Nogi's face remained impassive. His eyes stayed fixed on the shot glass of sake.

"You like being unemployed, I take it."

"I ought to flatten you for that."

"All right, you don't like being unemployed. You're just too yellow to fight back," Nogi challenged.

Lyons launched a loping, overhand right that a baby could intercept. Nogi's left arm drifted upward and back as if he were doing the backstroke. When the arm finished its stroke, Lyons's wrist was trapped under the karate expert's armpit, and the crook of Nogi's arm put pressure on the back of Lyons's elbow. When the Japanese slid off the bar stool, Lyons was forced to follow or have his arm broken. The small man grabbed his own wrist and increased the pressure on the arm, hustling Lyons out of the bar.

As they went out the door, Nogi spoke. "This is your last chance. Do you wish to learn to handle yourself better and be paid for it, or do you want to step into the alley with me for a demonstration?"

"You're not shitting me? I'd have a job?"

Nogi did not bother keeping the amusement out of his voice. "You'd have a job."

"Okay, boss, you got a man."

"You're willing to go through stiff training?" Nogi insisted.

"Let me go, will you? Why do we have to talk while you're breaking my damn arm?"

"I'm not breaking your arm. If I let go and you take a swing at me, then I will break your arm and you'll be no good to me. Is that clear?"

"Is what clear?"

Nogi carefully suppressed a sigh of exasperation. "I'll let you sleep off the alcohol and then we'll talk. No business until *I'm* sure you have a clear head. Is that understood?"

Lyons looked at the scuffed toe of the old construction boots he was wearing.

"I, uh, haven't had a chance to find a room yet."

Nogi grinned. "I thought not. That's okay. We provide our team with living quarters until they're well into training. Do you want to stay there, tonight?"

"You're not ribbing me about a job?"

"Not if you can leave alcohol alone and follow orders."

"I'm no damn wino."

"We'll soon know. I'll break both your arms if you are. Now, I'm letting go of you. You can come with me or go away, but take a swing at me and I'll break you into little pieces and leave you here. Is that clear?"

Lyons nodded slowly, reluctantly.

Nogi let go of him and began walking, leaving Lyons to come or go. Lyons followed, rubbing his shoulder.

"You were lucky," Lyons sulked. "You won't get me like that again."

Nogi kept walking at a brisk clip.

"Tell me that tomorrow in the dojo," he grated at the blowhard he had just recruited.

"The what?"

"The gymnasium, you long-nosed idiot."

"Why didn't you say so?"

Nogi continued in silence, wondering if he would have the restraint not to break this one into little pieces. The garbage he got to work with was hardly worth the trouble.

July 11, 805 hours, Smyrna, Georgia

THE RECEPTIONIST JUDGED that the two redheads were in their early thirties. She also guessed that both women had at one time been blond. The women, who introduced themselves as the Ross sisters, wore expensive business suits and carried attaché cases.

"Mr. Brognola will see you right away," the receptionist told them. "His assistant will take you to his office."

The elder redhead asked, "Who is Mr. Brognola? We've done much of the recruiting for Elwood Industries, but we haven't met him before."

"Mr. Brognola has taken over as acting manager since the disturbance," the receptionist answered. She was polite, but did not encourage further pumping.

The assistant appeared in the reception area.

"Susan, Jennifer, it's good to see you again," she said

to the recruiters. "I'll take you to Mr. Brognola's office."

Susan, who was four years older than Jennifer and looked ten years older, shook the assistant's hand. Jennifer gave the woman a hug.

"After the terrorists hit here, we've had some difficulty getting staff back together," the assistant said. "Mr. Fischer and his secretary were killed. Some people quit. Some say they're still too shaken to come back to work."

They passed a place where workmen were replacing a bullet-shattered door. The two sisters exchanged glances.

"So, I told Mr. Brognola that you could find the type of people he needs faster than anyone. I know the company, so I'm helping him find his way around."

When the two recruiters walked into the chief executive's office, they knew they had been recognized. But they could not recall ever having seen the gray-suited, gray-haired man who stood up and came around the desk to shake hands.

"Sit down, ladies. Would you like a coffee?"

Both shook their heads. They held their attaché cases tightly, knuckles white. Hal Brognola perched on the corner of his desk, studying the two women.

"How's Henry these days?" Brognola asked.

"Oh, he's the same as ever," Susan said. "I swear if I live to be a hundred, Henry will still be around and still be the same. We asked if he wanted to retire. He was really annoyed with us for...."

Her voice trailed off. Her face turned white. She looked at her sister who was holding her briefcase much too tightly.

"How do you know about Henry?" Jennifer demanded. There was anger and defiance in her voice.

Brognola smiled. "Relax. I'm a friend of a friend."

Neither women said anything. Their eyes were locked on Brognola and filled with suspicion.

"This friend," Brognola continued, "posed as an enforcer to get Jennifer out of the Sciaparelli house and then went back and carried Susan out."

"You wouldn't have had to know him to know that," Jennifer said. "It was in the damn papers."

"He told me some time later about how you kept the mobsters at bay. He said that his marksman medal exactly covers your navel."

Jennifer's paleness was suddenly transformed to a mild tint of pink. "That's something Mack Bolan had better have told only to a friend," she said.

"So what's happened to you two since then?" Brognola asked.

"At first we hid from the Mafia. There weren't that many left in this area to hide from," Susan answered. "Then, when we thought we were safe, some capo sent us word that the incident involving our father was over and done with. If we'd forget, so would they. We kept the last name change. It was pretty close to Rossiter anyway. We went into this type of headhunting and so far they haven't bothered us."

"You think the truce will last?" Brognola probed.

"Not a chance!" Jennifer replied.

"But we've given up running and hiding," her sister added. "When trouble comes, we'll meet it."

"I still miss Mack," Jennifer said softly.

"Why did he have to die in that damn explosion!" Susan exclaimed.

Brognola's heart ached to tell these two women that Mack Bolan still fought the good fight, still had to watch his back against those who should be helping him. But it would do neither Mack Bolan nor the United States any good to broadcast that the warrior was still very much alive. Brognola wanted to tell them, but he had to settle for a sigh.

The Rossiter sisters—now the Ross sisters—also sighed.

"Back to business," Brognola said, his voice brusque.

"What do you need?" Susan asked.

"Staff. At least temporary. Some will probably be taken on permanently when regular management takes over again. But I want this place busy and productive in three days."

"Three days. You're joking." Jennifer exclaimed.

Brognola shook his head.

The two recruiters looked at each other for a moment and then stood up.

"I'm sorry, Mr. Brognola," Susan said. "We're not interested in your business."

"We need those people."

"We're not in the habit of supplying live bait for traps," Jennifer said.

Brognola stared at them.

"The bait is Lao Ti," he said. "Routine jobs are being filled by federal agents. Everyone will be evacuated under protection of those agents, if there's any danger. No one is bait except her.

"We need people to really make this establishment run," Brognola added. "We can secretly pump some money in, but in these days of computer record keeping, we can't fake a productive company. We need the real thing. They'll be safe, but we'd be wasting our time without them.

"Trouble's here," Brognola told them. "Are you going to meet it, or run?"

The two recruiters paused for a second before answering.

"We'll do our best for you, but no guarantees," Jennifer said.

"I never ask for more than that," Brognola assured them.

July 11, 938 hours, Atlanta, Georgia

THE ATLANTA OFFICE of Workers Against Redundancy was in a building in one of the city's new industrial subdivisions. When Nogi had taken Lyons into the WAR office at about ten the previous evening, volunteers were still bustling, stuffing envelopes, filing, answering telephones.

Behind the general offices were a few executive offices. Nogi headed straight for a door marked President. A tough-looking individual in a security uniform sat at the secretary's desk. He nodded to Nogi and pressed a concealed buzzer, admitting them to the president's office.

Nogi walked through the empty office and used a key to open what appeared to be a closet door. Lyons followed him through that into the back half of the building, the world of the Harassment Initiation Team.

Nogi led him to a long room filled with double bunk beds. About two dozen were occupied; the same number were empty, a tribute to the effectiveness of Able Team. Nogi unlocked a supply room and loaded Lyons with bedding, a toothbrush, a disposable razor, and a karate *gi*, or fighting uniform, with a white belt.

"Wear these and report to the dojo with the rest, tomorrow morning," he ordered. He then left without another word.

Lyons considered exploring during the night but decided against it. He was willing to bet that someone was waiting for him to do just that.

Lyons took his sleep while he could get it. He made sure that he was neither the first man to do anything, nor the last. He rose, shaved, showered, and put on the supporter, *gi* and sandals provided.

"You're new?" someone asked.

"Last night. When do we eat?"

"Not until after the first workout."

Lyons cocked an eyebrow at the pimply youth who was speaking to him. The boy's yellow belt looked unsoiled. Lyons guessed that he had just been promoted from white and was feeling kindly disposed to lesser creatures.

"We have three workouts a day and one two-hour session in a classroom. How well you do determines how much time you get off. Each new belt means we get paid more money. Same thing goes for marksmanship.

"I'm afraid I'm never going to get a raise for my shooting," the yellow belt confessed.

Ever since Lyons had been given the *gi*, he had been chewing on the problem of going through karate classes without showing his own proficiency. Perhaps if he stuck close to the yellow belt and imitated his mistakes, he could cover himself.

"I'm not too bad with guns," Lyons said. "I'll give

you some tips, if you'll show me some of this judo stuff."

"First, it's not judo, it's karate. Don't let Mr. Nogi catch you making that mistake. He'll cuff you around and make you do fifty push-ups or sit-ups or something."

"That little Nip better keep his hands off me," Lyons muttered, thinking he had better get back into character.

Pimples turned pale. "Don't let him hear you say that," he whispered. "Mr. Nogi can smash bricks with his bare hands. He's murder on anyone who doesn't show the proper respect.

"Some guy failed to bow when he came into the dojo two days in a row. He beat him so thoroughly that the guy had to be taken to the hospital. We never saw him again, but you better believe everyone who saw that bows when Mr. Nogi comes in."

"Never saw the guy again," Lyons mused.

"Naw. He must have been booted out."

Probably buried, Lyons thought, but said nothing.

"You going to show me the ropes?" he asked.

"Ahh, we'll see. I got to go now."

The kid hurried away, leaving Lyons with a distinct impression that alliances in HIT depended on how favorably the candidate was viewed from above.

Lyons had to prevent himself from bowing to the dojo when he entered. No one had told him to do so; it would have been a giveaway. He took five paces into the large room with the bare floors before he was hit on the back of the head with sufficient force to throw him on his face.

"Bow when you enter a dojo," Nogi told him.

It would have been easy to slap the floor and roll when he was hit from behind, but Lyons knew that would give away his training. So he absorbed most of the fall with his arms. His palms stung and he was face down and helpless. Nogi placed his bare foot on the back of his neck and shoved his face into the floor.

"You bow when you enter a dojo, any dojo. Is that understood?"

Lyons twisted his head to one side. "What the hell are you talking about?" he asked.

Nogi kept his foot on Lyons's neck.

"Class," he called in an authoritative voice.

Lyons could see that mostly female students answered the master's call. He was surprised to see one platinum blonde, who looked as if she would be more at home in a massage parlor. She was looking at Lyons's face and smirking as she approached.

When the class was assembled, Nogi spoke.

"This worm was told to bow to the dojo. He has asked what the hell I am talking about. Because this is his first time here, I will be too lenient and explain. All of you listen. I shall not explain again."

"Are you going to let me up for the lesson?" Lyons asked.

Nogi put enough pressure on the neck to cause pain. "Shut up and stay where you belong, worm.

"Always you will bow to the dojo when you enter and when you leave. In future, you will receive a severe beating if you forget. I will not tolerate such disrespect. You will also bow whenever your *sensei* enters or leaves the room. You will also bow whenever a black belt enters and the *sensei* has not got your attention. Is that clear?"

Lyons said nothing.

Nogi pressed on his neck with his bare sole causing excruciating pain along the top of the vertebrae.

"It would be so easy to break your neck. Answer when spoken to."

"Yes, I understand," Lyons said. Inside he was telling himself that this was part of the price to pay for penetrating HIT.

"Here you answer the question by saying, *'Sensei!'* The tone of voice will tell me whether you mean 'yes,' 'no' or are asking a question. Can you grasp that, worm?"

"Sensei," Lyons grated. The foot eased slightly.

"You are still thinking of revenge. That is good. We like angry people here. They make fine fighters. Good luck with your revenge," Nogi said.

"Now I will tell you why you bow to the dojo, to the black belts, and above all to the *sensei*. The *sensei* has power, so you bow to that power. The black belts have acquired some of that power, so you bow out of respect for the power they have acquired. You bow to the dojo, because it is the place where power is transferred from master to student. Treat the dojo with respect because it is here that you will acquire the power which earns you respect.''

Lyons wondered how a person who had gone through the years of vigorous mental and physical discipline necessary to become proficient in the martial arts, could use that discipline to subjugate and terrorize others. As he thought, he relaxed.

Nogi took his relaxing as a sign of submission and removed his foot. Lyons remained on the floor until he was told to get up.

"Although we mix the sexes for training," Nogi announced, "I usually make it a practice to match training partners of the same sex."

He grabbed Lyons by the collar and flung him into the arms of the surprised platinum blonde.

"You two are partners, because women should train with women," Nogi said.

The blonde looked angry. The rest of the class tried to hold back laughter.

"Why do I get stuck with a *woman* who can't take care of herself?" the blonde demanded.

Nogi's tone was heavy with sarcasm. "You have showed me how great a warrior you are. I'm afraid to give you anyone more valuable. You might damage someone that matters."

When the laughter died down, Nogi added, "Take this worm and teach him fundamental manners and how to stand up. He seems to spend too much time on the floor."

The blonde shrugged and headed for one corner of the room. Lyons followed, content to be inside and in one piece.

6

July 12, 1004 hours, Santa Clara, California

Gadgets dropped the half-eaten doughnut back onto the table and stared morosely into his third cup of coffee.

"One of us should have gone with her," he told Politician for the fourth time.

"There's a chance someone in that building saw us in Atlanta," Pol said. "It's better if she cases the layout first."

Gadgets did not look convinced. He looked around the doughnut shop. No one was particularly interested in them. They both wore suits and ties and looked like two businessmen having a long meeting.

A soft voice spoke as a hand touched Gadgets's shoulder.

"I'm back," Lao Ti said. Gadgets shifted over in the booth and Ti slid in beside him.

"WAR has the second, third and fourth floors of that old office building," she reported to Pol and Gadgets. "The computer room is on the south side of the fourth floor. Excellent security. The building is full, but the tenants on the sixth floor, south side, are just moving in. Some sort of sales firm for personal computers. No one in this branch of WAR was in Atlanta at the time of the raid on Elwood."

"How did you find out all that?" Gadgets asked.

"It wasn't difficult. First, I went to the building superintendent and asked about renting. I learned from him that CompuSales had taken the last vacancy and were in the act of moving in.

"I went to CompuSales and applied for a job. From that

I learned the location of the office and the fact that they're new and can't afford to hire anyone.

"Next, I applied for a job as programmer at WAR. I learned the location of the computer area from the way the security is set up. Being an organization for the unemployed, WAR takes workers from its own ranks. I was invited to join. When I told them that I had worked last across the road from Elwood, they were full of questions. From the nature of the questions, I'm sure that no one has come from Atlanta to that office since the battle."

She ended with a small shrug. "So I spent all this time just applying for jobs and talking to people."

"Terrific job," Politician told her.

"What's next?" she asked.

"Next," Pol said, "we move into that office instead of CompuSales. Ti, you've been in there once and know the approximate setup. Go to a prestigious location and rent something that would suit them much better."

She nodded and waited for the rest of the plan.

"As soon as you have the location, telephone us at the new CompuSales office. Gadgets and I will be there waiting to tell them where they'll be moving to."

Ti left the booth without another word. Pol and Gadgets started down the block to meet the owners of the new computer business.

A young man in jeans and a T-shirt that read Love Bytes straightened up from the case he was unpacking and stared at Politician.

"You want us to do what?" he asked.

"Move to a better location where you'll have a better chance of making your business really work."

"We can't afford a better location," the only other member of the business, a bearded youth, said.

"Wrong. We'll give you the same lease you have here at the same price. We put up the difference, plus the moving costs. You won't be out anything more than the delay of half a day moving."

"Why this dump?" the youth with the beard asked.

Pol proceeded to feed them a story about how the people

they worked for had set their sights on that location, and that no other location would do.

Pol talked to Ti, then to the young businessman. "How's downtown sound? Same price."

The two men grinned at each other.

"What are you guys?" the man with the T-shirt asked. "Tooth fairies?"

"Deal," said the other.

Able Team was in business.

"Where is this better location?" the youth in the T-shirt asked.

The telephone rang.

"If that's for me, I'll tell you where," Politician answered.

That night Lao Ti looked around the empty office. "We could use some furniture," she commented.

"Order some in the morning," Gadgets replied. "In the meantime, what's the first step?"

"The telephones," she answered. She stooped and rummaged in an open case. "I brought a switchboard along."

Gadgets looked at his watch. "The super and the cleaning staff will be gone by now. Let's get it done."

There were still people moving around in some of the WAR offices. Otherwise the building was deserted. The trio found the door to the basement. Its lock yielded to Gadgets's hands and a piece of spring wire. Soon they were in the basement, examining the junction boxes and spaghetti that controlled telephone service to the building.

Ti quickly clipped a handset to one pair of wires after another.

"No action on the lines," she reported. "We'll have to do something about that. Pol, if you can, find a place where there are five pay phones close together. Go down the line and dial the first six digits of WAR's telephone number. Then go down the line a second time and dial the last digit. That should light up all their lines and speed up the process."

Gadgets and Ti hurried to connect small light bulbs and circuit testers to the wire sets.

Ten minutes later, lights flashed and needles moved. Both Ti and Gadgets moved quickly, tagging the active lines with bits of tape.

"I've found the trunk," Ti announced. "Two of the lines in it didn't light up. I'll bet one of those is hooked up to the computer."

Half an hour later, the three were back in their new offices. Ti pointed to a compact switchboard that she had just hooked up.

She explained to Politician: "All their calls go through that board. We can record everything that goes through the lines, but I still want to patch directly into their mainframe. Otherwise someone is bound to notice the increased activity through the modem."

Pol shook his head. "We'll never get through that security and back out without them knowing we've been at their computers."

"So, they'll have to invite us in."

"Sure."

"We monitor those two unknown lines until one starts to transmit to the computer. As soon as the transmission starts, whoever's monitoring throws the switch that opens the line, cutting them off in the middle. After that, it should be easy."

Pol shrugged. "If you say so."

They dragged sleeping bags out and settled in on the bare floor. Gadgets took the first four-hour watch on the telephone lines.

Nothing came into the computer modem until shortly after noon the next day. Ti was monitoring at the time. Her hands fluttered over the small switchboard, breaking open telephone lines, routing outgoing calls to the three telephones she had spread around the floor of the empty office. At 12:25, an outgoing call rang one of the telephones. An automatic LED display showed the number that had been dialed.

"This is it," she said calmly as she picked up the telephone. "Repair service," she said into the mouthpiece.

Gadgets came and flipped other circuits to allow the office below them the usual telephone service. The important call had been intercepted. The computer line was left dead.

"Hold on for a moment, please," Ti told the caller from WAR.

She grinned at Pol and Gadgets, letting the caller wait ninety seconds before going back on the line. "We have a repairman in the building, now. I've talked to him. He'll look at your problem as soon as he's finished the job he's working on now."

She hung up.

"You're up next," Ti told Pol.

He stood and started to change into appropriate clothes.

Twenty minutes later, toolbox in hand, Pol was ushered into the computer room and to the area where the mainframe was hooked into the telephone line. Pol carefully set out his tools and began dissecting the modem. The two men who had ushered him into the computer room sat down to keep an eye on him.

"Before I get too deeply into this I'd better do a line check," he said when he had the modem into easily reassembled sections.

He pulled a lineman's handset from the toolbox, hooked it up and dialed a seven-digit number. Pol knew that the number did not matter because Ti would intercept the call.

"Yes?" Ti's voice was carefully neutral.

"Just checking on the line. Everything here looks okay. Call me back on...." He paused and raised a gray eyebrow at one of the watchers.

The watcher left and soon returned with a slip of paper on which he had written the computer's unlisted number. Pol relayed it to Ti and hung up.

Twenty seconds later, his handset rang. Pol answered. "Are you still being carefully watched?" Ti asked.

"That's about it."

"Gadgets wants to know if some smoke would help."

"Seems like we should do that," Pol acknowledged.

"Ten minutes," Ti told him and hung up.

Pol continued to pretend to work on the computer

modem. A few minutes later, he smelled smoke. He kept busy, waiting for someone else to notice it.

By the time someone did, there was a noticeable amount seeping under the door to the hall.

"You smell something?" someone asked.

"Look," said one of the men guarding Pol.

The two guards made for the hall door while the rest of the staff gathered around. The guards looked into the hall.

"It's only a smoldering wastebasket. Somebody's playing tricks. I'll take care of this. You get back to the repairman," one guard told the other.

Attention was off Pol for only ten seconds. That was sufficient. He whipped a pressure can of self-setting Styrofoam out of his toolbox, shoved the nozzle into one of the vents on the side of the computer mainframe and squirted for five seconds. The spray can was back in the toolbox before anyone's attention returned to the repairman.

Politician carefully reassembled the modem.

"That should do it," he announced. "Care to give it a try?"

A computer operator was called over. She telephoned Seattle and told them to try their transmission again. In twenty more minutes, she pronounced everything in order and Pol left.

Politician went back upstairs and reported to Gadgets and Ti.

"Terrific," Gadgets said. "The computer should go down in two or three hours."

"If that foam is going to take the computer out, why didn't it take it out right away?" Pol asked.

"The Styrofoam isn't conductive," Gadgets explained. "It doesn't affect the computer directly, but transistors generate heat, and if there isn't sufficient cooling they fry themselves."

"So the computer has to operate for a while to build up enough heat to cook the circuit boards," Pol concluded.

"That's right. Now, we wait and intercept the next repair call."

"We have to prepare. Let's hope the computer lasts a

few hours," Ti reminded Gadgets. She then got the computer's make and description from Pol.

"It would be best to buy the entire computer," Gadgets suggested. "Then Pol can show us where he squirted the foam and we can figure which circuit boards will be cooked."

Ti agreed.

Gadgets took off on a shopping expedition. The computer went down before he returned, but Ti just promised them service within the hour.

When Gadgets finally lugged the six cubic feet of mainframe into the office, Ti was intercepting the second call to see why the serviceman was not there. She assured them he was on his way.

Once the cover was off the central processing unit, it was easy to see which circuit board was going to be out of service. Gadgets quickly removed several and put them into his toolbox. He put on a pair of yellow coveralls and left.

Gadgets took the elevator to the main floor. When the door opened, he found the lobby milling with people.

"Anyone here know where the office of Workers Against Redundancy is?" Gadgets shouted.

A hard case looked him over, took in the toolboxes that looked like attaché cases. "You the computer repairman?" he asked.

Gadgets nodded.

The hard guy stepped on to the elevator. "Where you been?"

"Getting misplaced," Gadgets answered. "What floor?"

The WAR man hit the button for the fourth floor. "I thought I'd see you coming in," he remarked.

"What's wrong with the computer?" Gadgets asked.

"Hell, I don't know. I'm part of the security detail."

They arrived at the fourth floor. The hard case led the way.

Once on the spot, Gadgets opened one of the attaché cases and went to work. The security man found a chair and sat to watch.

Gadgets raised part of the metal cover, slid his hand under and lifted the blob of Styrofoam with the cover. That safely out of the way, he took out a tester and probed here and there.

When one of the computer operators went past, Gadgets asked some questions about the malfunction.

"This section was overloaded and is on the modem regulation part of the board," he said. "Did you have modem trouble late yesterday?"

The computer operator was impressed. "Actually we only found out about the defective modem today. It could have gone out late yesterday. We wouldn't have caught it until information came in today."

Gadgets nodded. "No problem. I have a spare board with me. I'll rewire slightly so this can't happen again."

"Terrific," the operator replied and went away, content to have Gadgets working on both the computer and the modem.

Forty minutes later, he was done. The computer would operate normally, but Lao Ti had direct terminal access through extra telephone lines.

"Our problems are over," Gadgets told the security guard while putting tools away. "Call us if you do have more trouble, but the way I've set that up, you won't be worrying about the computer."

"Yeah. Thanks," the security man replied.

The HIT man found a buddy and they accompanied Gadgets to the elevator. The Able Team member pressed the down button. As soon as the elevator doors were closed, he pressed the button for the second floor. He got off on the second floor. No one was in sight. He went to the stairs and walked up to the sixth floor.

The two HIT men were waiting for him.

"See," said the one Gadgets had met in the lobby. "I told you this guy got off an elevator from this floor."

"How do you explain that, buddy?" the other one asked.

Gadgets looked perplexed. "Of course I came from this floor. That's where my last call was. I left my time sheets in there and I need them. Excuse me." He started to shoulder past the HIT security man.

The second one looked puzzled, but the first one was more sure of himself. He placed a hand on Gadgets's chest.

"Not so fast. I don't believe you."

"If you got a problem, take it up with the company. In the meantime, I have to get my invoice book and write up the parts I put on your damn computer. Now, will you get out of my way?"

"Sure. You don't mind if we follow you to this office where you say you made your last call?"

Gadgets dropped the cases and attacked.

Before the cases hit the floor, Gadgets's fist was striking into one solar plexus. His victim doubled over as Gadgets turned toward the other hardman who had started to claw for a weapon at the small of his back. He never managed to get the weapon out. Gadgets drove a foot into his crotch, then followed with a knuckle to the temple. The goon dropped in a dead heap. Gadgets returned his attention to the creep who was doubled up and fighting to breathe. He wrapped his arms around the goon's neck. A sudden tightening of the arms caused a gross cracking sound. The man let out a moan before he dropped to the floor.

Gadgets opened the door to the office where Pol and Ti waited.

"Help me clean up," he said.

Gadgets quickly gathered the tools from the one attaché case that had popped open while Ti and Pol each dragged a body into the empty office.

"What happened?" Pol asked once they were inside the office.

"One of them was too sharp. He noticed I got off from an elevator that came from this floor. So, he brought his friend along and they were waiting for me when I doubled back up the stairs."

"How soon do you think they'll be missed?" Pol asked.

"Too soon. They have a good security system. I figure

these two will be missed and people will start looking for them within half an hour. If they think we'll be out of the office at a definite time, they will probably wait until then to search here.''

"Sounds reasonable," Pol agreed. "But if they come to the door, we all stand a high risk of being recognized.''

"Speak for yourself," Ti told him. "I'm ninety-eight percent safe from recognition. To the sharp-eyed Westerner one Oriental looks like another.''

"Don't count on it," Pol answered.

"If someone comes to that door, we have no choice but to count on it,'' she answered.

Pol opened the window and looked out. "This building looks like it was built in the thirties—ledges, funny carvings, stones on the corners, the whole works.''

Gadgets hurried to the window. "Let me look.''

He hung out the window for a couple of minutes. He brought his head back in. "I know what we'll do. We'll return the bodies.''

Pol and Ti just stared at him.

"The window to the computer room is down two floors and over two sets of windows. If we lower someone on a rope, they can go along the ledge to the window. We break in and return their bodies. That gets rid of one problem. The. . . .''

"That ledge is only decoration. It's only four inches wide," Pol interrupted. "No one could walk the thirty feet along that to the windows of the computer room.''

"We both know someone who could," Gadgets replied. "And we both know she has the guts to do it.''

Pol grinned. "And we both know how much you're aching to see Babette Pavlovski again, but there must be some way that we can handle it ourselves.''

"There's dozens of ways we can handle this ourselves. The problem is to handle this and keep the cover on this operation at the same time. All our work is wasted if they find we've tapped into their computer.''

Pol paced the floor for a few minutes without speaking.

He sighed. "You better call your lady to come up from L.A.," he told Gadgets.

Then he turned to Ti. "While he does that, I'll stack these bodies in the closet. Can you get that telephone and computer somewhere where it can't be seen from the door?"

She looked around the bare room.

"How about inside one of the boxes?"

"Let's do it. Time may be limited."

7

"Just feather stroke the trigger and let it up as quickly as possible," Lyons instructed. "These M-16s have only thirty rounds in a full magazine. It tosses them out the end of the barrel at the rate of eight hundred rounds per minute. Figure it out. That's only two and a quarter seconds of firepower. If you don't want to be killed while changing clips, make the ammunition last. You can kill an unarmed civilian with just one bullet, and if you line up children maybe you could make one bullet do for two."

The blonde who had been given Lyons as a partner, looked at him quizzically. She had treated him with barely suppressed contempt when showing him the basic stances of karate. She had found him an almost impossible pupil when it came to the etiquette of the dojo, but on the firing range it was different. This Carl Leggit—the name Lyons had chosen to go by—proved to be a better shot than the instructors. Quickly he was made a gun instructor and his karate partner was his first pupil.

"Okay, Deborah, try it again," Lyons told her.

"What's this crack about children?" she demanded.

"Who the hell do you think you'll be killing? Trained combat infantry? Armed riot squads? Hell no! If it can shoot back, stay away. We're terrorists now. We shoot only those who can't defend themselves."

Deborah Devine, a platinum blonde with warm blue eyes, shuddered and moved a little farther from Lyons.

One of the white belts appeared in the firing range in his *gi*. He ran down the line of trainees. "Everyone change and get back into the dojo right away," he called. "Everyone change into *gi* and go back to the dojo right away.''

Ten minutes later, Lyons was standing in the dojo, lined up behind Deborah. This was the way of Nogi's dojo. Every pupil above white belt was assigned to help at least one pupil of a lower rank. So by grouping instructors and students the lines formed naturally, black belts closest to Nogi, the browns next to the blacks they were assigned to, the blues standing close to the brown belts who were responsible for them. This order filled the back ranks with white belts. Deborah wore a blue belt and was the only one not assigned one or two greens. Instead she had Lyons in his white belt to follow her around.

Lyons still did not know what Deborah had done to cause Nogi's displeasure. Although she was intelligent and attractive, Nogi seemed to take great delight in humiliating her.

When Nogi entered everyone bowed. Lyons was glad to bow and keep his grin toward the floor—he knew he had struck gold. A wide, ugly Japanese woman followed Nogi into the dojo. She wore a well-used *gi* and white belt. Her hair was pulled together and tied, like a samurai's of two centuries ago. Everything about her shouted her deadliness. This could only be the female terrorist leader whom Lao Ti had described.

Lyons knew that the white belt was not worn because the woman was a beginner at karate. It was traditional for a *karateka* who was visiting another dojo and did not wish to usurp the authority of those who were running it, to wear a white belt.

Nogi did not have to hold up his arms to gain attention. A karate *sensei* always has his students' attention. Nogi had only to begin speaking.

''Aya Jishin does us the honor to visit us again. Most of you do not need to be told who she is, but for the new recruits I will say that she is the very capable commander of all the Harassment Initiation Teams. She brings us another chance to strike out against those who have taken your jobs away from you.''

No one cheered. No one smiled. Everyone simply transferred attention to the ugly woman.

Lyons's attention almost wandered as her monotonous hoarse voice reminded people of how they had been victimized by automation. He listened more attentively when she got down to the specifics of the operation.

"We attacked Elwood Electronic Industries four days ago, killing many of the enemies of the worker. However, the biggest enemy, Lao Ti, escaped. Tomorrow we will go back and find her and execute her in the name of the millions of unemployed."

She had Lyons's full attention now. His adrenaline was racing. Hal Brognola was setting that place up as a trap, but he would not be set yet, not by a long way. Somehow, Lyons had to get the raid postponed until they could get set.

"Question," Lyons called out in a loud voice.

A sudden silence fell over the dojo. No one had interrupted with a question before.

Jishin looked at Nogi, her glance demanding that he explain how such a thing could happen.

"He started yesterday," Nogi reported. "He can shoot the testicles off a flea at a hundred yards, but he has no civilized skills or understanding at all."

"You had better teach him some elementary manners soon," Jishin remarked. Her voice was hoarse at the best of times; in her anger it sounded like a bullfrog trying to talk.

"Question," Lyons repeated.

"What is it?" Jishin snapped, her voice menacing.

"According to the newspapers, you lost your entire squad the last time you hit that place. Wouldn't it be more sensible to learn if this enemy of yours is there *before* you go in and throw away another squad?"

The members of the Harassment Initiation Team started to mutter to each other. Since it was their lives on the line, it seemed to make sense that the person they wanted should be there when they attacked.

"Do you take us for complete fools?" Jishin demanded.

"That depends on whether you've bothered to get enough intelligence. Do you know when whoever you want will be there?"

"You doubt my ability to do things properly?" Jishin raged.

"After the last fiasco. . . ." Lyons replied with a shrug.

"Teach him some manners, *now*," Jishin commanded Nogi.

The karate instructor glided to the centre of the dojo and motioned to Lyons.

"All this crap because I recommend the use of basic strategy," Lyons bitched as he sauntered toward the *sensei*.

Lyons was to be made an example for all those under Nogi's guidance. The idea was to make the beating short, swift, savage. Later, when there was no one to see, the victim could be killed and disposed of. The class would be told that he was too ashamed to come back.

Nogi faked a blow to the head and drove his foot toward the Able Team member's crotch. Lyons's closed fist connected with the shin bone with enough force to spin Nogi on his one foot, deflecting the front kick to one side.

Nogi backed up very quickly and stood for a moment, sizing up his disciple. Lyons stood waiting. He adopted no particular stance, deliberately looking casual, but his weight was well distributed and he was ready to react instantly. Lyons knew that he had one small advantage to offset Nogi's lifetime of training. Nogi was forced to bring the fight to him.

"You would dare to strike your *sensei*?" Nogi said, his voice indicating that no one in his right mind would do such a thing.

"Of course I'll try to defend myself if the bastard attacks me," Lyons spat.

"It's hopeless," Nogi told him.

"Get on with it," Jishin commanded from the sidelines.

"You always listen to that stupid old lady?" Lyons asked.

Nogi answered by advancing one long pace at a time, flashing out a kick or a punch with each step forward. It would have been deadly, but Lyons stepped sideways or backward each time Nogi came forward. He retreated twenty feet. None of the blows connected. Someone snickered.

Angrily, Nogi increased his forward charge. Lyons delivered a short uppercut with his right fist to Nogi's elbow, causing the karate master's blow to go high in the air. Lyons's left fist slammed into the exposed ribs with the impact of a HE grenade. Ribs cracked.

Again Lyons did not try to press his advantage. He was out of the fight and away before one of Nogi's killer fists or feet could launch another blow.

The karate instructor was no longer a coolheaded adversary. He was losing face, and anger and humiliation combined to push him into desperate maneuvers. He rushed forward with a flurry of front kicks.

Lyons backpedaled, leaving Nogi to kick hell out of empty space. The tempo increased. A lifetime of practice meant that Nogi could move forward kicking faster than the big blond could backpedal.

Lyons suddenly reversed direction, plowing straight into the instructor between kicks. He landed a hard blow to the chest. In return he received an elbow smash that sent him reeling. Nogi waited until Lyons staggered away the right distance. Then the foot flew up again. If it had connected with the plexus where it was aimed, it would have killed. However, Lyons managed to twist. The kick glanced off his ribs, sending him whirling like a top.

Lyons knew he would not have time to recover his balance, so he harnessed his circular motion and spun back into the battle. He twisted past a flashing foot and landed a light blow to the side of Nogi's neck. Lyons stood, his body pressing against the terrorist's, his arms working like driving pistons on an engine. Nogi was blocking the constant rain of body blows, but could not free an arm to strike back, nor could he lift a leg to kick. If a leg came off the floor, the force of the blows would have upset the Japanese *karateka*.

Nogi went low to the ground, his feet braced so that he was stable and difficult to upset. Then he exploded upward. Lyons was pushed back, once more fighting for his balance. Nogi moved in immediately, snapping punches.

Lyons found himself covering up, trying to backpedal,

but forever off balance. He finally managed to fall back into a deep cat stance, most of his weight on his left leg. Up to this point, Lyons had given no indication that he too was a *shotokan* karate black belt. He had fought like a street-wise tough, but street methods were only good for their surprise value.

Before Nogi could recognize Lyons's trained stance, the terror fighter's left foot flashed up in a high front kick that smashed the instructor back three steps before he fell on his ass.

Nogi was caught by surprise. He had made the fatal error of underestimating the man he fought. The moment it took Nogi to readjust his thinking was the time it took Lyons to move forward and snap another kick into Nogi's chest. The sound of breaking bones could be heard.

Nogi did his best to roll away from the assault. His broken ribs slowed him down. Before he could get his foot under him, another kick rolled him farther. Then a roundhouse kick to the side of the head jarred him almost into unconsciousness. With an effort that came from deep conditioning, rather than from conscious thought, Nogi managed to wrap one arm around the flashing leg and hang on. The fighters found themselves tangled on the floor.

Nogi tried for a short, hard punch to Lyons's crotch. He succeeded only in bruising the side of the thigh. The leg that he had hit flew up and caught him in the face. Before Nogi could recover, large arms had wrapped around his head, forcing it painfully to one side.

Lyons risked a quick glance at Jishin. She had recovered her calm and was watching the fight with clinical interest.

"Finish him," she said.

Before Lyons could react to the order, one way or the other, Nogi made a desperate bid to break the killing hold. He kicked both feet in the air and twisted his body to relieve the pressure on his neck and spine. Lyons moved both arms toward the floor in a quick, sudden motion. Nogi did not twist in time. His neck snapped.

Lyons immediately released the head and stood up slowly, wondering where the next attack would come from.

Jishin sighed.

"I should have recognized your quality and taken on your discipline myself. We are even. You insulted me by severely underestimating my ability and I insulted you by doing the same."

Lyons nodded. The words meant nothing to him, but if she chose to talk rather than have all her killers close in on him, that was fine.

"I understand you have taken over gun instruction."

Lyons nodded again.

"Do you also want the post of unarmed combat instructor? You seem to have proven your ability in that department as well."

"Depends," Lyons answered.

"On what?"

"On two things. What does it pay? And what are you going to do about my suggestion that you get more intelligence before you act. It was bad enough when I was worried about my own neck. But if I'm responsible for training these people, I don't want them thrown away."

It was a good speech. The others in the dojo felt that Lyons was looking out for them. He was winning their minds from Jishin. She was no fool. She could see that clearly.

"Salary is something to be discussed in private," she answered. "But your other point does you credit. Just the fact that you are willing to speak up in defense of those who have been put in your charge, makes you much more valuable to me. Exactly what do you suggest we do?"

Lyons was surprised by her political adroitness. She moved to the side of protecting the troops without appearing to have moved at all.

"I suggest someone go to Elwood Industries and find out whether this Lao Ti is there."

"Then do it. We will continue this meeting when you get back."

Lyons turned to go.

"Take your partner," Jishin told him. "We always use the buddy system when scouting."

Lyons kept the disappointment off his face, nodded to Deborah, and stalked to the door.

Just as Lyons turned to bow to the dojo, Jishin spoke again. "You had better bring your partner back in good health, and she had better be able to account for every second of your time. Otherwise you are dead."

Lyons nodded, bowed and left.

Jishin watched the pair leave. She then turned her glance to Nogi. She was glad to see his body there. He had caused her to lose more face than necessary in her fight with Dr. Lao. She signaled to three of the black belts. They were longtime terrorists who knew better than to indulge in false heroics. When they gathered around her, she spoke to them in a voice too low for the others to hear.

"Follow those two. If they do what they are sent to do, we'll kill them during the raid. If they try to run, or to contact another person, kill them."

The three nodded and ran to change into street clothes. They were confident that they would be ready before the man and woman.

8

During the afternoon only one person poked his head inside of the office where Ti, Gadgets and Politician waited.

"Setting up?" he had asked.

"Waiting for the movers," Ti replied, and he had gone away.

It was almost a quarter to nine in the evening when there was a loud rapping on the door. Pol and Gadgets slid against the wall behind the door, leaving Ti to handle whoever was there. If someone forced their way into the room, it would be easy to spot the Able Team warriors, but there was nowhere else to hide.

Ti saw a solid, smoothly muscled woman who stood five-foot ten. She had fine blond hair, cut short. Behind Babette stood two brawny individuals. One had his hand around the woman's elbow.

"Babette!" Ti shrilled. "It's so good of you to come and keep me company."

Ti threw herself into the strange woman's arms.

Babette's left arm tore free of the goon's grip and wrapped itself around Lao Ti.

"No problem. How long do you figure you'll have to wait?"

Lao, who had no idea how Babette would react, breathed a sigh of relief before answering. "The boss says that if the moving truck isn't here by ten, I might as well lock up."

"You girls going to be here until ten?" one of the HIT men asked.

"Don't get any ideas," Babette said coldly.

"Aw, nah. Nothing like that. We'll keep an eye open for you, that's all," the man answered.

"Thank you," Babette said in a cold voice. "I'm sure we can manage."

She stepped inside, turned and closed the door. Immediately she saw Pol and Gadgets hiding against the wall.

Ti put her ear to the door to hear if the two men were moving away. Soon she heard the elevator and risked opening the door. They were gone. She looked back to report, but found Babette and Gadgets in a tight clinch.

"Is it best out of three falls, or can anyone take on the winner?" Ti asked.

Gadgets and Babette, close friends since Able Team's last mission, started laughing.

Ti took a long, up-and-down look at Babette.

"How can anyone so large do what you need?" she asked.

Babette laughed. "Don't you know? Large women are more fun."

"Wasn't quite what she had in mind," Gadgets told Babette. "We have some bodies to get rid of. We're hoping you can walk a small ledge to a window."

Babette immediately got down to business. "Show me," she said.

Gadgets took her to the window and showed her the ledge.

"We need to get a rope in the other window," he explained.

Babette pulled her head inside. "It's no problem," she said. "Just a matter of keeping my center of gravity within five inches of the building. Do we start now?"

"Let's wait until it gets a shade darker," Pol suggested. "I bought some good nylon line, and pitons to drive into the mortar...."

Half an hour later, Schwarz and Blancanales carefully lowered Babette two floors. The rope was tied under her arms about the center of its length. She kept the excess coiled over her shoulder. As she descended she kept her arms and legs out to keep from spinning on the end of the rope.

When Babette's heels hit the ledge at the fourth floor, she seized the rope and brought her arms straight in front of her, forcing her body back, flat against the building. Slowly and cautiously she resettled her feet so that her heels were tight against the building face. Then she signaled for slack in the rope.

Pol and Gadgets played out the rope with smooth teamwork. Never was more than one of the four hands off the thin nylon line. Ti stood by the office door, prepared to deal with unwelcome visitors.

Babette kept her knees slightly flexed to keep her weight as far back as possible. She slid her left leg out eight inches and then brought her right leg in eight inches. She looked as if her spine was held to the building by a strong magnet.

When she reached the window she carefully removed a mirror from the front pocket of her slacks. She held this so she could inspect the interior of the computer room. After carefully scanning the inside of the room, Babette began the process of moving back along the ledge. When under the window where Pol and Gadgets waited, she signaled to be hoisted up.

Once back inside the office, Babette reported. "My two friends who escorted me up here are sitting in the computer room. They seem to be alone, but they have a walkie-talkie nearby. I would guess that they're waiting for us to leave before they start to search the building."

"We have to get them out of there before they lose patience," Politician pointed out.

"How?" Ti asked.

"The perfect solution is to distract them while the bodies go in the window, and then just leave," Pol said after a moment's silence. "Let *them* explain how the bodies got into the computer installation they were guarding."

There was another long silence.

Babette suddenly brightened. "If I secure the hook in the window, can you three move the bodies down? And if I unhook the window from the inside, can you move quietly enough to hide the bodies?"

"I can handle that," Ti said.

Babette turned to Gadgets. "I need a portable tape recorder and some slow sexy music."

Gadgets looked at his watch. "There's still time to get that from the corner store."

"I'll go," Ti volunteered.

"Okay," Babette said, "get those. When you get back I will go down to the goons' office and distract those two. You'll stash your garbage and get back out. Make sure you get me a tape player with lots of volume."

As Babette went back out the window, Lao Ti went to make the purchases. She moved through the halls quietly and met no one. She was relieved to see that the cleaners were still in the building. It meant that the HIT operatives would not start to search until the cleaners left.

Once more Babette was lowered two floors to the ledge on the fourth floor. She carefully crabbed along the ledge to the window of the computer installation. After checking the inside of the room, she crossed over the window and made her way farther along the ledge. It was a tricky operation that had the two men sweating. They had to slack the rope away off so it would not dangle in front of the window. If Babette slipped, she would fall a long way before the slack was out of the rope. They did not know if they could hold on.

Once she was sufficiently past the WAR offices so that the noise would not be heard inside, Babette drove the pitons into the brickwork, working slowly, carefully, concentrating on keeping her center of gravity within the narrow limits of the ledge. Then she had to lean forward enough to free the loose rope from over her shoulder. The next job was to tie the end to the pitons. The job had to be done well, but could be done only with one hand. It was slow work and the concentration required was similar to what she needed as an Olympic gymnast—which she was as a youth—or an Olympic-caliber coach, which she was now.

On the way back along the ledge, Babette had to check the computer-room window with the mirror in her right hand. She saw two heads turned toward the clock on the wall. A sense of urgency gripped her. She began to pick up the pace. The result was that she held her arms too far from her body as she passed the mirror from her right hand back to her left. Her center of gravity shifted beyond the edge of the thin ledge. She almost fell. Babette shot her arms out in front of her as quickly as her highly trained muscles could react. She then continued the motion until her hands hit the wall over her head.

The momentum of pushing her arms out pushed her back against the wall. Before her body could lose balance again, the arms were against the wall over her head. She breathed deeply and slowly slid her arms down along the wall to her side. It was then that she realized that the mirror had dropped out onto the street. She watched carefully for a moment, but no one had noticed.

Pol and Gadgets pulled Babette in the window. They all breathed deep sighs of relief.

When Lao returned, everyone got back to business. Babette pawed through the half-dozen tapes that Lao had bought. Gadgets put the batteries into the portable stereo. Pol dragged bodies from the closet.

"I don't see why they call this portable," Gadgets remarked. "It must weigh twenty pounds."

Lao shrugged. "She wanted lots of volume. This one can break eardrums."

"Hey. This is it. This is exactly what I wanted!" Babette exclaimed, holding up a cassette.

"What are you going to do with it?" Pol asked.

"I'm going to deliver a message, a message that will keep those two downstairs totally occupied for over four minutes."

"Can we get two bodies down there in four minutes and then get out?" Pol asked.

"It should be easy," Gadgets figured. "We'll already have a rope sling on them. We'll tie the rope off and use it to slide the bodies down to the other window. I'll catch them there and haul them in. If Ti watches my back, it should be easy.''

Pol turned to Babette. "How will we know when to start?"

"When you see the window open, start down there. When you hear the music, get moving. I'll play it loudly. It'll cover any sound you make.''

Gadgets stared at her for a moment. Her electric-blue eyes met his without flinching.

"You'll be taking a bigger risk than walking narrow ledges,'' he told her. "How will you get back out of there? I imagine they'll want you to stay and play.''

"If she isn't out of there one minute after the music stops, I'll go in after her,'' Ti said. "I can get her out without anyone associating us with their main problem.''

Gadgets grinned at the small woman. "Do that,'' he agreed.

"Give me a couple more tapes to drop into my handbag,'' Babette said to Gadgets.

"Which ones?''

"Doesn't matter. It just wouldn't look right if I carried a monstrosity like this and didn't have several tapes to paw through.''

Pol grinned. "This lady knows role camouflage.''

"Let's put the show on the road,'' Gadgets said.

Babette hefted the oversized portable and let herself out of the bare office. Ti waited a few seconds and then followed. Pol and Gadgets were already preparing to move the bodies down two floors.

Gadgets looked up from the grisly task and chuckled. "Good thing the streetlights don't reach this high and that there's no moon yet. I'd hate to have to explain to some cop what we're doing right now.''

Pol tied off the rope, being careful to get the slack exactly right so that the line would take whoever was on it to the fourth-floor ledge just outside the correct window.

"You ready for your space walk, commander?'' he said when he was finished.

"As long as I have firm footing,'' Gadgets replied, looking out the window.

BABETTE KNOCKED TIMIDLY on the door to the WAR computer room. In a moment it opened a crack.

Babette put on an easy grin. "Hi," she said. "Can I use your telephone?"

"Don't you have one upstairs?" The voice was curt, impatient.

"I don't know. I wouldn't use it anyway. Some calls a girl doesn't want another girl to hear."

The HIT man was curious. "If you used our phone, we'd hear you," he probed.

Babette made a gesture with her left hand, dismissing the thought. "That doesn't count. You don't even know me."

The eye made an up-and-down movement. At least that much of the man was trying to get to know her better. After a couple of seconds the door swung open.

"Sure, come in and call," the guy decided.

As Babette entered, the other hardguy glanced up from a desk where he had been playing showdown with his partner. His eyes fixed on the cassette player.

"You didn't have that when you came in here," he said.

"Nah," Babette answered. "I loaned it to my friend, but I need it back. I use it for my work."

"You must be popular with the boss if you take that damn thing to work."

"You don't get it. The boss supplies them. The girls got to make a deposit, you know, but then we get to keep the thing as long as we work there."

The tough crumb was interested. "Work where?" he asked.

"Very Special Message."

"What special message?"

"Nah. That's the name of the place I work, Very Special Message. You got a message you want delivered it can be delivered by a gorilla, a clown, Santa Claus. But mostly people order strip-a-grams. No one ever sent you a strip-a-gram?"

"You mean you go and do a striptease to deliver a message?" the guy who let her in exclaimed.

"Sure. No one ever sent you a strip-a-gram?"

"Who'd send *me* one of those?"

"Your boss. Your girlfriend. Just about anybody with fifty bucks and a sense of humor."

The two hardguys looked at each other. They were both grinning.

"Hey fellas, I came in to use the phone, remember?"

The guy sitting at the desk said, "I don't remember, but I'm sure you could deliver a message."

"Hey, have a heart! This is my night off."

"Why don't you have a heart, baby."

"Yeah," agreed the one who had let her in. "I've never seen a strip-a-gram."

"You're kidding," Babette said. "I've done so many of the damn things that I'd of sworn everyone has seen me personally. And Bernie has ten of us going full-time, plus some part-timers in the busy season."

"Let's see you do your thing, kid," said the man at the desk. It sounded more like a command than a request.

"I ain't dressed for it," Babette complained, but her whine indicated she wanted to be encouraged.

"I thought you got undressed for it," the seated guy scoffed.

"I could just go down and use the lousy pay phone," Babette complained. "But you guys were so nice, making sure I found the right place. I'll see what I can do. It's too hot in here. Open the window. This is hard work."

"The place is air-conditioned."

"Listen. One rule we have is no sex—we're not prostitutes. The second rule is: if the place is hot, we don't do it. We can't shower after and we can't afford to go home between every message. So, either I open the windows, or I go use the pay phone."

"Go ahead. We can close them later."

Babette walked over to the windows and opened them. Her slow controlled walk already had the men excited. Hers was the perfectly conditioned, perfectly balanced body of the highly trained athlete. It was exciting every time she moved.

She then went back to the door area and arranged chairs for the two men.

They took the seats with their backs to the window.

Babette rummaged around in her handbag.

After seeming to debate over a couple of tapes, she put on the sound track for *Flashdance* and quickly found "I'll Be Here Where the Heart Is." She pretended to be making up her mind, listening to part of it, deliberately building the suspense and the tension.

She then turned up the volume and stood up, poised, balanced. Babette moved in perfect time to the slow music. Her audience was unaware that what they were really seeing was a slow version of her daily warm-up exercises, stretching and warming every muscle.

As the song moved into the second verse, Gadgets let himself into the room. Babette had locked eyes with one of the men. She kicked her shoes into his chest so he had to catch them.

Gadgets turned his back on the scene and leaned out the window. Before the verse was over, he was dragging the first body over the window ledge.

Babette locked eyes on the really hard case and played with the buttons on her shirt. They came undone with agonizing slowness. Her victim's eyes were riveted on the shirtfront. He was scarcely breathing. One of the corpse's heels hit the floor with a slight thump, barely audible above the sound of the stereo. Gadgets quickly looked around, but neither man had noticed. He decided that he could probably set firecrackers off behind them without attracting attention.

Babette's shirt slipped from her shoulders. Every move was slow, sensuous. Both men were leaning forward.

Gadgets looked around and spotted an office he could reach without coming into the audience's peripheral-vision range. He yanked the rope off the arms and hoisted the body to his shoulders, moving silently through the computer area.

The third verse was playing as he made his way back. Gadgets found it almost impossible not to stop and stare.

Babette was fondling herself in time to the music. The muscles on the men's necks were knotted from excitement. Gadgets forced himself to turn his back and lean out the window. He took a deep breath of air before signaling to Politician to slide the next body down the rope.

The body accelerated through two stories of almost free-fall. Gadgets braced himself and wrapped one arm around it. The force tore his grip loose from the window ledge, but he managed to stop the body by catching his feet on the window ledge. The problem was to get himself back in without letting go of the 160 pounds of dead weight.

Politician saw what was happening. He put on a pair of gloves and then wrapped himself around the rope and quickly slid down. The song was through the second chorus and on to the fourth verse.

Gadgets glanced over his shoulder. The men were about to fall out of their chairs as Babette slowly slid off her slacks.

Between Politician and Gadgets, the body was quickly hauled into the computer room. Politician took one glance at Babette, then hastily turned his face. He and Gadgets carried the body between them.

The last chorus was playing as the two members of Able Team crept back to the window. Babette was strutting back and forth, clad only in a pair of bikini briefs.

Gadgets climbed out as the chorus began to repeat and fade out. There was no time to undo the rope, Politician was already climbing.

Gadgets took up the slack rope in his left hand—he had his knife in the right—and edged onto the ledge toward the pitons. He slashed the rope as far from the window as he could reach. Then, as he lost his balance, he dropped the knife into his pocket and grabbed the rope with two hands.

The rope was nearly taut because of Politician's weight. Gadgets was swinging at a high speed past the face of the building. He put his foot out and bounced himself out from the wall. As gravity pulled him back toward the wall, he managed to get his feet up to absorb the impact. He got himself braced, facing upward, with his feet on the brick surface.

The two worked their way up slowly, hand over hand, to the office two floors above.

Inside the computer room the music faded and Babette froze in an inviting pose with her arms spread open.

"Terrific," enthused the one who had let her in.

"Ahhh, you didn't finish the act," said the other, pointing to the bikini panties she was still wearing.

Babette reached for her shirt. "I went a hell of a lot further than I ever went before. We're supposed to stop at bra and panties. And usually we have another set of skin-coloreds on under those."

The tough one stood up and seized her wrist. He pointed to the sheath, still strapped to her forearm.

"And what the hell is this?" he growled.

Suddenly Babette's voice was no longer friendly. There was steel in it. "It's an ice pick. It reminds the customer that this is only a show."

Her hard voice was punctuated by an authoritative pounding on the door, and Ti's voice. "Babette, are you in there?"

Babette wrenched her wrist out of the tough's grip and proceeded to put her shirt on while she glared at him. Then there was a thump, the door flew open; the jamb was splintered at the catch. Ti stood in the hall, her foot still in the air from the powerful side kick that had sent the door crashing open.

The two men stood staring, unwilling to believe that such a large kick had come from such a small woman. Babette stepped into her slacks.

Before the two hardmen could speak, Ti snarled. "What's going on here? What were you doing to her?"

"We weren't doing nothing to her," one whined.

The other broke into a grin. "I think we're being treated to a new version of the badger game," he told his companion.

Babette picked up her handbag and the cassette player. She started for the door.

"Take it easy," she told Ti. "They were only being friendly, until I started saying no. Some guys just don't know where the line is."

"Not so fast," said the toughest one.

Babette whirled on him. She seemed to be on the verge of tears. "It was fun until you had to get so damn grabby. Why can't you be a nice joe, like your friend?"

She slipped through the door and ran down the hall, her shoulders shaking.

The two men turned toward each other with puzzled expressions.

"What's she crying for?" one asked.

"Don't ask me. They're the last from the building. Let's get to work."

Gadgets and Pol were waiting in the shadows by the front door of the building. Babette came out first, her shoulders shaking with laughter. A few seconds later, Ti followed, her wide mouth split into an impish grin.

"Won't they find your computer when they search the office?" Babette asked as they wandered down the street.

"They're looking for bodies. All offices have computers," Ti answered. "There's no way of telling that it's monitoring their computer and telephone lines. They won't give it a second thought."

"I wonder if they'll associate us with the bodies in their own office," Babette persisted.

Politician grinned. "I doubt it. It doesn't look like they'll discover the bodies themselves. What I wonder is how they'll explain those bodies, or if they'll even be given a chance to explain."

"How long are you going to be around?" Babette asked.

Gadgets sighed. "About another hour. We'll be leaving for the airport as soon as we have something to eat."

Babette still had questions. "What happens to the office?"

"The computer runs it," Ti explained. "I have it on a telephone modem. I can call it from anywhere. It will dump a high-speed report into another computer and carry out any monitoring or control of the WAR computer that I tell it to. We won't have to go near that office again. The only problem will be if the HIT people discover what's happening.''

"Why don't I look in once a day to see if anything's been disturbed?" Babette suggested.

"What about your coaching?" Pol asked.

"I'm still on post-Olympic holidays. After all, even athletes relax for short periods."

Ti handed Babette the key to the office. "Best if you check during the day. That way you're unlikely to meet your boyfriends again. They're less apt to try anything if you do."

Babette took the key and nodded. Then she sighed.

"Well, if a girl has to settle for just food, it had better be a good meal."

9

Lyons had to credit Deborah Devine—she did not take forever to dress. He showered, shaved and put on jeans, a jean jacket and a plaid shirt in his customary twelve minutes. At that, she was waiting for him in the lobby of the building.

Her hair, still damp from the shower, was pulled into a long ponytail. She wore slacks, a silk blouse and sensible walking shoes.

As they left the building, Lyons noticed a man, still buttoning his shirt, come around from behind the building. He wondered how many other goons had been sent to keep an eye on him. It was a problem. He could do nothing to arouse their suspicion, but he would have to ditch them, so that he could warn Brognola about the impending attack. He was not worried about the blonde at his side. Brognola would find some way to separate them when they reached Elwood Electronics.

"Let's take a taxi," Lyons suggested.

He steered them toward Fulton Industrial Boulevard, hoping to flag a cab there. Deborah did not move particularly quickly. She decided it was time to check how she looked. Lyons swore as she pulled a mirror out of her handbag. Then he noticed that she was not really looking at herself—the mirror was doing a scan. He filed the information.

They had no luck finding a cab and soon found themselves walking to the nearest bus line. Lyons itched to look back, but he did not want to make his companion suspicious.

Half an hour later, they were in downtown Atlanta. Soon they would find a bus headed for Marietta, which would drop them in Smyrna, within walking distance of Elwood Electronic Industries.

"I wanna stop and eat," Deborah said.

Lyons thought about that. He had picked out only one tail, sitting three seats behind them on the bus. Lyons could not crane his neck trying to spot the car he was sure would be following them without giving himself away. Stopping to eat would give him a chance to spot and ditch whoever was following them.

"Sure," he agreed. "Let's get off here."

"There's no restaurant around here," she complained as he led the way to the door.

"We'll find one."

The tail walked to the front of the bus in order to keep his back to them. His technique was so clumsy that Lyons was sure he was there simply to be ditched.

They got off at a corner and started walking down the longest block he could find. Their tail wagged himself after them.

"You sure picked a tough part of town to take a stroll in," Deborah complained.

Lyons was looking for a way through to the next block. In the middle of the next block, he found exactly what he was looking for. A narrow gap between two buildings served as a walkway from the parking lot behind to the front of the building. Beyond the parking lot was the entrance from the next street. A car would have to go around the block to pick them up and Lyons could spot whoever followed them on foot.

"Through here," he grunted, picking up the pace.

He turned his head as he spoke. A man was hesitating at the mouth of the walkway. Lyons could not see enough from the corner of his eye to make an identification. He then caught sight of Deborah's face. She was eyeing him.

The parking lot was sheltered by buildings on four sides with just two lanes for entry and exit. In its secluded confines they ran into trouble. Six punks were stripping two cars and stowing the loot in the back of a van. Two other punks held switchblades on the elderly parking attendant.

Lyons's Colt Python rode a pancake holster in the small of his back, but drawing it would probably get the old attendant sliced. He turned his steps toward the attendant's booth, pretending not to notice the gang stripping the two cars.

"Get out of the way," he commanded Devine in a voice that would not carry.

She nodded and drifted off between the cars.

Lyons approached the booth as if he was oblivious to everything but his own thoughts. He rummaged around in his pockets, searching.

"I have my monthly pass here, somewhere," he muttered to the attendant.

The street gang was one of the few that had achieved integration. One of the attendant's tormentors was a blond fair-skinned youth, the other looked as if he was of Puerto Rican origin.

The blond youth snickered. "Yeah, sucker. Your ticket's just been canceled." His knife came away from the old man's throat and pointed at Lyons.

Lyons looked at the speaker as if seeing him for the first time. He was about twenty, thin, but tough looking. He then looked at the Puerto Rican punk. With a growl the goon slashed at Lyons's face.

The Able Team member's left hand clamped on the Puerto Rican's knife wrist, his right hand came up behind the elbow, forcing it straight. He used the punk's stiff arm to lever him into his buddy, who was knocked back three paces before he knew what was happening.

A sudden amount of extra pressure on the wrist snapped it like a dry twig. The knife fell to the asphalt. Lyons pushed back on the arm and let go. The punk staggered back a step. Lyons executed a snap kick to the crotch that introduced his opponent to a new world, one where nothing existed except pain.

The blond hood came in fast, his knife low and weaving. A grin of cruel satisfaction decorated his face.

"You gonna die slow," he told Lyons.

Lyons turned. The knife-wielder charged, straight into a back kick that broke his forearm and dumped him on his ass. Before he could figure what had hit him, a roundhouse kick to the temple relieved him of the necessity of ever figuring anything out again.

One of the youths who had been stripping a car stepped out from between the parked cars. He held a Saturday night special in a professional-looking two-handed grip.

"See how good you are at kicking bullets," the gunman sneered.

Lyons was in the open, too far from the gunman to reach him. Deborah Devine materialized between the cars, behind the gunman.

She grabbed his right shoulder with her left hand and pulled. At the same time she stomped hard into the back of the thug's right knee. The knee buckled and the gun was jerked to the side, its bullet flattening a tire on the car beside Deborah and her prey.

As the man turned, Deborah grabbed his gun wrist. With leverage on both his shoulder and his wrist, the would-be killer was easy prey to the curvy blonde. She twisted him around until his head met the corner of the car windshield with a solid whack. The gunman screamed in agony. The gun fell from his fingers. She shifted her left hand from his shoulder to his greasy hair. The head was smashed into the corner post once more. Devine let go of the unconscious form, picked up the gun and ran over to Lyons.

The thug's scream had alerted the rest of the gang. They abandoned the cars and came running. There were five of them. Two had revolvers, one had an automatic. The other two sported switchblades.

Deborah held the captured gun in a two-handed firing-range stance.

Lyons shot the gang member whose revolver was closest to being lined up on target.

The 158-grain wad cutter slammed into the punk's chest, stopping him dead. The two cannibals behind him were sprayed by the half pound of flesh that was shredded away from the exit wound.

Panic caused the animal with the automatic to fire prematurely. The Browning BDA .380 kicked and spewed its death seed into the air. Deborah's captured gun barked back and the punk spun away with the impact of a .38 in his shoulder.

What was left of the gang took off in a sprint for survival.

Deborah dropped the .38 into her purse as the parking-lot attendant walked up to Lyons.

"Thanks, mister," he said. "I thought I was gone."

"You're welcome," Lyons grunted.

The old man surveyed the dead punks. "I'll have the cops pick up the litter. They'll want to ask you some questions."

"Sorry, friend. I've got things to do. Just tell them that a pair of concerned citizens gave you some moral support."

Lyons and Deborah strolled toward the street. There was no use hurrying. Whoever had followed them had lots of time to set up both exits from the secluded parking lot.

Lyons spotted a grungy cafeteria in the middle of the next block.

"Still hungry?" he asked.

She nodded.

HE MECHANICALLY BEGAN EATING. "So what made you decide to help butcher people who work for computer firms?" Lyons asked around a mouthful of meat loaf.

Deborah finished chewing her mouthful of sandwich before answering. "I used to earn four hundred dollars a week as a stripper."

"Paint, film or clothes?" Lyons asked. He stared straight ahead while they talked, never looking at her. He shoveled in the food.

"Uhhh, clothes. No one ever thought I might be some

other kind of stripper. You're the first who ever asked me a question like that.''

"So what happened?''

"You ever notice how many fewer burlesque houses there are over the last five years? It's the video games that do it. Even the Roxy where I worked for years, is now a video-game parlor. If it weren't for those damn computers and all those silly games, I'd still be employed.''

Lyons continued to feed himself and stare straight ahead.

"You really believe that crap?'' he asked.

"You haven't told me about yourself,'' she said, changing the subject. "Do you know that you're the first man I've been with who hasn't told me how important he is?''

"Then you've been with assholes,'' Lyons snapped.

They finished eating in silence.

"Great food,'' he said. "Now, it's time to get to work.''

"How do you plan on getting into Elwood and searching around?'' Devine asked.

"I've got a plan,'' Lyons replied.

He led the way to the street in a leisurely pace. Immediately he spotted a tail in a battered pickup. A scrawny character with a scar over one cheek was at the wheel. Lyons proceeded until he came to a pay phone. He looked up the number to the building department in city hall and placed a call, asking for a building inspector.

In a hoarse voice, he conned the inspector. "Hey, I'm a straight Gyproc man. I don't go for this cheating on buildings. I don't want no part of it.''

"What are you talking about?'' the inspector asked.

"Having to pull every second stud out of walls, before putting the Gyproc up.''

"Where is this happening?''

"Ah, hell. Never mind. With my luck you'd use a magnet or something. Forget it.''

"What do you mean use a magnet?''

"Those stud finders you use actually are small magnets. They don't find the wood. They find the nails. Whenever a stud is pulled, some nails are put through the Gyproc anyway.''

Lyons hesitated. "Hell, if you meet me right away, I'll go to the site with you and show you which walls to inspect, but no one can see me. I got to work for those people again, and I gotta keep my union membership."

The building inspector was all fired up to be a hero. He took the location and said he would be there in twenty minutes.

"What the hell are you up to?" Deborah asked when Lyons hung up.

"We need identification and transportation. The city is about to provide it. When that inspector gets here, I want you to distract him."

Twenty minutes later, the city inspector pulled his two-year-old Ford up to the curb alongside a large blond man, who stood with his back to the road and refused to turn around. The city employee honked his horn. When that produced no noticeable reaction, he climbed from the car and approached the man.

Before he reached Lyons, he was intercepted by a stunning blonde with a blockbuster figure.

"Could you tell me where Parsons Street is?" she asked.

He turned to her to direct her. At that moment the large blond man turned and struck him under the ear. The inspector's knees buckled. Before he could fall, the blond man had him by the coat collar and the belt. The beautiful woman opened the back door of the car and the man dumped the unconscious city employee inside. They then climbed into the car and drove away.

"This is better," Lyons said. "Do you know how to find Smyrna?"

"Take 285 to the Cobb Parkway. What are you going to do with that inspector?"

"We should kill him, but for now just get me his wallet," Lyons, playing the role of Carl Leggit, said.

Deborah leaned over the back of the front seat and fished into the unconscious man's jacket pocket.

"I want a cut of this guy's money," she said.

"I want the entire damn wallet, but first check to make

sure the ID is there and it doesn't have a photograph attached. That ID's going to get us into Elwood."

"There's a photograph," she reported.

"Then I'm going to have to flash it only once and so damn fast no one can see a thing. That's okay, though. If there's a photograph, people assume you wouldn't dare use someone else's ID."

"You're kidding."

"Just watch."

They arrived at Elwood Electronic Industries twenty minutes later. As they climbed out of the car, Deborah nodded her head toward the back seat.

"What about him?" she asked.

"He'll sleep for another half hour. By then, we'll be gone."

The receptionist looked up politely. Her smile was warm, but her eyes held the calculating look of a prospective mother-in-law sizing up the engagement ring.

"Who's in charge here?" Lyons demanded in a gruff voice.

"Mr. Brognola, but if you've no appointment. . . ."

"Would you please tell him that John Ironman is here to do the annual building inspection?"

"Do you have identification, Mr. Ironman?"

"Of course I have identification, and I'll show it to Brognola. Now, buzz him."

The receptionist looked as if she was tempted to move around her desk and personally eject John Ironman, but she restrained herself and placed a call instead.

"Mr. Brognola will be right out."

"Thanks."

Hal Brognola appeared in the reception area twenty seconds later. He wore a gray suit.

"Mr. Ironman?"

"I'm here to do the annual building safety inspection," Lyons said. He passed the stolen wallet in front of Brognola's eyes so quickly that no one could have discerned a thing.

The new manager of Elwood Electronic Industries

seemed more interested in the inspection than the inspector.

"I'm fairly new here. Just what are you looking for? And will you require any assistance?" Brognola probed, hoping Lyons could slip some clues into the conversation.

"Just looking for anything that might constitute an immediate safety violation. Don't worry, our function is to advise you of unsafe conditions, not to issue a summons or anything. If we find things unsafe we return today or tomorrow and see if you've remedied the situation. We always figure that cooperation is better than attack."

"That seems very logical. What can I do to cooperate?"

"Not much. I certainly don't need three or four shadows following me around. Your people can stick to their own jobs. Miss Devine, my assistant, is the only observer I need."

Brognola nodded, his face bland except for a slight hardening of the muscles around his mouth.

"Then I'll tend to business. Let me know what you find. I'll be in my office in about half an hour. I'll wait until I see you again."

"Okay," Lyons answered.

"By the way," Brognola asked, "how's traffic along the parkway?"

"Not bad. I have one of those Fords that the city provides. I managed to get here without putting a ding in the fender. It's hard to explain that you totaled another car because of some battered GMC pickup that you didn't see."

The acting chief-executive officer of Elwood Electronics shook his head as he left the reception area. "Amazing," he muttered.

"What's so amazing about getting here without an accident?" Deborah wanted to know.

"With you to look at, it's a miracle that I could spare any attention for the road," Lyons told her.

She ignored his flattery. "Weird," she commented. "What do we do now, Mr. Inspector."

Lyons led her out of earshot of the receptionist, before answering. "We inspect. We go through every square foot of the place until we're certain that this scientist is either here or not here. You have her description?''

"Of course. I was given it at the same time you were, remember?''

"Just barely."

"Then let's start inspecting, inspector."

HAL BROGNOLA HURRIED away from Lyons. He had been uncertain how the big blond would handle the undercover work. No one ever really knew what Lyons would do next. However, there was no doubting the communications, in spite of the witnesses who were watching and listening.

Brognola went over the points in his mind. "Advise you of unsafe conditions" and "return today or tomorrow" could only mean that Lyons had come to scout the place for another attack by HIT, but what were the conditions? Hopefully Lyons could clarify that before he left the building.

"Three or four shadows" when Miss Devine was the only assistant he needed was also clear. Brognola hustled into his office and locked the door behind him. He pulled out a sports bag filled with tools of the trade.

He slipped off his jacket and put on a soft-leather, breakaway shoulder harness. He checked the clip on a Heckler & Koch VP 70Z. The eighteen 9mm parabellums were all waiting for action. He slammed the clip home, making sure it was seated. Then he clamped a stubby sound suppressor over the end of the barrel, tightening small set screws into the thumb grooves on the side and front of the gun barrel.

With the suppressor and the internal spring mechanism that delayed the shell ejection, the automatic weighed almost three pounds. He slipped the deadly German-made gun into the clip under his armpit and then put his jacket back on. The impeccable tailoring hid the presence of the gun very well.

Brognola rummaged in his sports bag until he found a weighted cosh, which he slipped into his left pocket. He unlocked his office door and headed for a side-door exit.

"I'm stepping out for a breath of air. I'll be back in ten minutes," he told his secretary.

It took no time to find the battered GMC pickup on the company lot, but there was no one with it. That gave Brognola the problem of finding the terrorists who were probably spread out watching all the entrances to the building. After a moment's thought he went to his rented Chrysler.

He started the car and drove carefully through the lot until he came to the pickup truck. He stepped his speed up to about twelve miles per hour and steered the heavy car into the front fender of the truck. The impact was exactly right. It curled the fender into the tire so the truck could not be driven until the fender was straightened or removed. The high-impact bumper on the New Yorker absorbed most of the shock. The crumpling of the fender did poke out one headlight, but Brognola noticed no body damage when he got out and looked.

It took only eight seconds for a thin man with a knife scar on his left cheek to make his appearance.

"Why the hell don't you watch where you're driving?" the man demanded in a whiny voice.

"I did," Brognola assured him. "I hit exactly where I aimed. The trouble is that tinny fender didn't crumple as it should. It broke one of my headlights."

"You did what?"

"I saw that disgraceful piece of garbage on a private lot, where it has no right to be. So I decided to disable it. Now it can't be driven away without slicing up the tire. I didn't count on breaking a headlight. I think you're going to pay for that."

"You think I'm going to do what!"

Another man drifted over to check the cause of the disturbance. He was a beefy character, dressed in jeans and cowboy boots. He needed a shave.

"What's the trouble, Kelby?" the newcomer asked.

"This asshole ran into my truck deliberately."

"Well, he's seen you now. We'll have to take care of him."

Brognola felt an uneasy prickle across the back of his scalp. These two would be too easy. That meant there were one or two others out there, and if they knew what they were doing, their guns would be trained on him right now.

Brognola turned and ran, pulling the VP 70Z as he threaded his way between cars, bending almost double to present a smaller target.

Two bullets came from a low angle and bounced off the roof of a car. Brognola caught sight of the only other terrorist from the corner of his eye. He let his knees buckle as if he was hit. As soon as he was below the rooflines of the cars, he turned and waited.

The fat goon in cowboy boots appeared first. He had run less than fifty feet, but was already puffing. Two parabellums tore into the terrorist's chest. He dropped in a pool of death.

Brognola changed position slowly, duck walking and listening as he went. He kept down and zigzagged toward the spot he last saw the gunman who had shot at him. He could hear the scar-faced terrorist scuffing tarmac as he tried to sneak up on the place where the Fed had dropped from sight.

Brognola went flat on his stomach, aimed his weapon and waited. Soon scar face's scuffed shoes came into view two cars down. Brognola put a bullet through each ankle and scrambled away quickly. Two bullets ricocheted off the parking-lot surface inches from his retreating legs. Brognola knew he was not the only one to think about shooting under cars. The whine of the bullets were lost in the screams of the man with two shattered ankles.

Brognola put his head close to the ground. He saw no one, so he took a few quick steps closer to the screaming man. He paused next to a set of tires and looked below the cars again. Proceeding in that way, he reached the wounded terrorist.

"Tell me who sent you or I take out your kneecaps as well," Brognola told the terrorist.

"They'll kill me if I say anything," the man gasped

through his panic. He was still in too much shock to feel the pain.

"And you'll never walk again if you don't," Brognola told him in a loud voice.

Two more shots rang out. Both bullets jarred the fallen man's head. He had been shut up forever by one of his own kind.

Brognola leaped from the ground to the hood of the nearest car, and from there to the roof. Each step took him in the direction of the sound of the last shots.

The angle worked to Brognola's advantage. He saw the top of the terrorist's head before the terrorist had straightened enough to line his gun up on the bouncing Fed. The VP 70Z coughed again. A small neat hole appeared in the top of the terror monger's head, and much of the back of the skull disappeared in a fine spray of red.

Brognola looked around. No one had been close enough to pay attention to the shots. Working quickly, he carried the bodies to the battered pickup and tossed them in the back. Luck was with him when he found a tarp in the truck and did not have to search for something to throw over the bodies. He then put the Chrysler back in its parking spot and pulled a suitcase from the trunk.

It did not take much hunting to find the Ford car with the building inspector in the back. The man was just regaining consciousness.

"You okay?" the Fed asked as he helped the man to his feet.

"Groggy as hell. What happened?"

"Did a large man knock you out and steal your car?"

The building inspector nodded. "Yeah. That's right. I remember him now. Wait until I get that son of a bitch."

"I'm afraid someone beat you to it," Brognola told him. He led the city employee to the battered pickup truck and raised the tarpaulin from the dead men's feet.

"His idea wasn't too bright. He got killed trying it."

"Trying what?" the inspector asked.

Brognola showed his Justice Department credentials. "You'd really be better off not knowing," he told the man. "Shall I arrange for a doctor to look at you? I really think you're fine, but I wouldn't want you to worry."

"I'm fine. Really, I'm fine."

Brognola seized the other man's hand and shook it.

The inspector drove out of the parking lot.

Brognola picked up his suitcase and went inside. He went past his secretary with the knees of his pants scuffed. "Slight accident in the parking lot," he explained. "Nothing serious."

Once again he latched the office door. He peeled off the abraded suit and put on another from the suitcase. He reloaded his weapon and continued to wear it.

LYONS AND DEVINE met in the cross corridor.

"No sign of a small Oriental woman. No sign of any Oriental women for that matter," Deborah reported.

"You check the washrooms?"

"Of course. Can you think of any way of telling if she's usually here and just gone for the day?" Deborah asked.

"We weren't told to go around asking questions. That would be risky," Lyons cautioned her. "Let's just go report to this Brognola sap and get out of here."

"Why don't we just get out of here?"

"Arouse less suspicion this way."

They found their way to the president's office. The secretary looked at them expectantly.

"Mr. Brognola said we were to see him when we finished the inspection," Deborah explained.

"He's expecting you. Go right in," the secretary told them.

"Well, Mr. Ironman, how safe is our building?" Brognola asked.

"Clean. No problems," Lyons reported. "Just keep things shipshape and you won't have any problems from me."

"Good. Then that will make two of us who have no problems. When will you visit next?"

"Oh, we'll probably catch you by surprise someday when you're having tea and don't expect us."

"We'll try not to get too slack, Mr. Ironman."

The three shook hands. Devine and Lyons left.

"You were good," Deborah whispered as they headed for the front door.

"It's all in the way you hold your sneer," Lyons confided as he reached for the door.

The door swung inward to meet his hand. He held the door open while Gadgets, Politician and Ti swarmed in.

Before any of them could react, Lyons snarled. "Watch where the hell you're going."

"Sorry," Ti said.

Lyons grabbed Deborah's arm and stalked out. They went to where they had left the building inspector and his car. Both were gone.

"Damn!" Carl Leggit exclaimed. "He came to and took off. We better get out of here."

10

July 12, 1742 hours, Atlanta, Georgia

Lyons and Deborah had to walk almost a mile before they were able to flag a taxi. The walk was made in heavy silence. Lyons had no doubt that Devine had spotted Ti, but could think of no reasonable way of asking her to forget it.

"Where to?" the cabby asked.

"Peachtree Plaza," Lyons grunted.

The two passengers settled back in stony silence. After a while the quiet began to irritate the driver.

As they passed a construction site, he piped up. "Atlanta must be the most rebuilt city in history. Did you know that no part of our skyline is the same as it was in 1970?"

His question was greeted with more silence.

"The hotel where you're going, that's the tallest building in Atlanta. Even that little park they have inside is eight stories high."

More silence.

"You folks already know the city, huh?"

"What city?" Lyons growled.

The cabby gave up.

Lyons paid off the driver and started to saunter along Cain Street. Deborah walked beside him.

"How come we didn't take the cab all the way to headquarters?" she asked.

"And leave a wide trail for anyone who wants to trace us from Elwood?"

"Why here?" she asked.

Lyons had told the cabby to let them off at Peachtree Plaza because it was close to the bus depot where he planned to catch another taxi to the industrial section where WAR and its terrorist arm, HIT, had their headquarters. Instead of saying so, he took a poke at Deborah's preoccupation.

"Thought we'd spend the night in the tallest building in the city. Nothing like having an indoor park."

"Okay," Deborah replied. Then she made a break for it.

Lyons could not afford to lose her. First, if she beat him back to HIT headquarters and let them know that Lao Ti was at Elwood, he could do nothing to stop the raid from taking place before Brognola was braced for it. Second, Lyons would not dare to show up in front of Jishin not able to account for Deborah Devine's whereabouts.

Lyons barely managed to keep her in sight. She was in good condition and fast on her feet. She seemed better able to steer through the late-rush-hour crush. He followed her for two blocks before finding a sidewalk sufficiently free of pedestrians that he managed to gain ground. She glanced over her shoulder, spotted him and quickly turned into a new building.

The skyscraper was another new hotel, not yet ready to be opened to the public. Lyons paused just inside the door, looking for Deborah. He wondered how Atlantians knew which building they were in. This one had all the usual features of Atlanta architecture, including glass-walled elevators and an acre of forest glade in the middle of the lobby.

Lyons guessed that the construction workers were using a back or side door and that someone had left the front door to the lobby open by mistake. Whoever's carelessness it was, it probably meant that Devine would get away.

Lyons was about to cross the lobby when he heard a rustle under one of the dogwood shrubs. He plunged into the foliage.

A foot shot out and kicked his legs out from under him. At the same time, a small fist tried to catch him on the vulnerable spot behind the ear. He rolled as he fell and grabbed the wrist just behind the fist. His other hand grabbed the arm above the elbow. He could have locked the elbow and dislocated something as he rolled. Instead he allowed the arm to bend and tossed Deborah across the path of his fall.

Lyons hit on his back. The freshly dug soil was as soft as falling on a mattress. Deborah tucked and rolled like a ball, flattening a patch of plants. Lyons lunged after her, staining the knees of his slacks. He caught her ankle and dragged on it before she could regain her feet.

"Hey, *officer*, we're on the same side," Lyons grunted.

She took a swipe at his head with her closed fist. He managed to deflect the hand upward with his elbow.

Lyons twisted her foot. She was forced to roll onto her stomach. Her hands scraped up fistfuls of soft dirt trying to find something to pull on. In the midst of her frantic clawing, she stopped.

"What did you say?" she asked suddenly.

She had propped herself on her right elbow and was looking over her shoulder and down the length of her leg to where Lyons lay, one hand on her ankle and the other on her foot. Lyons was grinning at her. There was genuine amusement in the usually icy eyes.

"I reminded you that we're on the same side."

"What side?"

"Well, it's this way, officer."

"Where do you get this officer jazz? Do you think you're in the Army?"

He let go of her foot and sat up.

"Yeah. It's a dirty war, but we're on the same side—trying to rid the world of a few more terrorist scum."

She was cautious, examining the words, looking for some indication of whether they were a trap.

"What gave you the idea that I'm some sort of cop?"

Lyons rolled his eyes. "Oh lady, are you ever some sort of cop. The looks you gave me had me uncertain right to the moment you lured me into your little jungle here and jumped me."

"Can I have my foot back?"

Lyons let go of her foot, pushed his hands into the rich

loam and brought both feet under himself. He was prepared to spring, if she took off or tried attacking him again.

She did neither. She rolled onto her back, then sat up. She pulled her knees up to her chest and wrapped her arms around her legs. She sat there, staring at Lyons.

"You say you weren't sure. That means you were suspicious," she said.

"Yeah. You gave yourself away in a lot of little ways, but I didn't see how you'd be trusted to keep an eye on me, if you were that obvious. So, I thought maybe you were testing me. How come they trust you so completely?"

"They don't trust me at all. That's why we were followed. Put your rotten fruit in a separate basket so it won't affect the rest," she said. "How did I give myself away?"

"You're too calm, too sure of yourself. And the way you handled that gunman in the parking lot. That was a takedown usually taught in police academies and seldom elsewhere."

"You mean I should have been more nervous?"

"No, Deborah...nice name that...but what do your friends call you?"

She hesitated for a moment and then smiled, almost shyly. "My friends call me Dibs."

"Well, Dibs, I gave you some severe pokes about killing the defenseless. All it did was make you try to figure out what sort of a nut I am. A terrorist reacts with anger when you suggest that they pick only on easy targets."

"I thought you must be insane. I bought it, when you told me that you enjoyed hurting people."

"I don't enjoy making anything suffer, but I will if I must. That doesn't mean I'm sane, just effective."

"You make weird jokes," she told him. "What kind of a cop are you?"

"The deadly type."

She searched his face to see signs of laughter. She did not find any.

"What kind of a cop are you?" he asked.

"State. We've spent months and I'm the first one to get

inside a Harassment Initiation Team, but I can't say I'm a trusted team member.''

"Even less so, after we return without our tails.''

"What happened to them?" she asked.

"I imagine they were taken care of before they could take care of us.''

She shuddered. "Why take care of us? We're following orders.''

"Some undercover cop. You do nothing but follow orders, huh?''

"Well, as far as HIT is concerned.''

"Don't underestimate them. Those were professional terrorists following us around. Jishin wouldn't waste their energy just to give us backup.''

Deborah shuddered. "You make it sound like we should be under this earth and not on it.''

"Let's just say we're into it, but still kicking.''

She put her forearms on his shoulders. Her hands nervously twisted the hair on the back of his head. She locked eyes with Lyons.

"Don't get me wrong. I volunteered for this. I wouldn't back out if I were offered the chance, but God! I *want* to continue kicking!''

"Of course.''

He wrapped an arm around her and pulled her into his lap. Her arms went around him.

"Only those who believe that life is precious risk their own lives to defend it. So, of course you don't want to die. People with death wishes find easier ways to fulfill them.''

She rested her head on his shoulder.

"We'd better get back to the war,'' Lyons said after a long silence.

She slid off his lap onto her back. Her arms stayed around him and pulled him down on top of her.

"Let's remind ourselves we're alive,'' she whispered.

Lyons laughed. He *knew* he was alive.

When they finished making love, when their energy abated, they lay sweating, and panting, tangled in the midst of a huge circle of ruined shrubbery and flowers.

Later they found an employee lavatory with running water. After ten minutes of washing and brushing, they were as presentable as they were going to get. Deborah used the opportunity to telephone in a report.

As the two wandered out of the lobby, Lyons looked back at the desolated jungle.

"People should really be more careful about locking doors," he muttered.

11

July 12, 1905 hours, Smyrna, Georgia

Hal Brognola leaned back in the comfortable leather chair
behind the desk in the president's office at Elwood Electronic Industries. He sipped black coffee from a mug and
looked across the rim at Lao Ti. She was sitting in a chair
in front of the desk, her legs tucked under her. There was a
pot of tea on a side table close by and she held a handleless,
Japanese teacup.

"What are Gadgets and Pol up to?" he asked.

"They're double checking my security arrangements. I
don't think they quite trust me, yet."

"They never fully trust anyone. It goes with the territory. They even check out each other whenever there's
time. That's the way they stay alive."

Ti nodded. "Of course. *Bushido*, the way of the warrior, dictates vigilance all of the time, but I always thought
that was theory. I've never seen it in practice before."

"It's rare, because the price is high," Hal reflected.
"You see it only where lives are always on the line. I imagine Miyamoto Musashi understood it very well."

Ti grinned at Hal's reference to the "Sword Saint" of
Japan.

Brognola took another sip of coffee and then got down
to business. "How ready are we for another terrorist attack?"

"An attack will be difficult for us to handle. We hold
'fire drills' to evacuate people quickly from the building,
but I think everyone's figured out that they're attack drills.
When someone asks what to do if the terrorists show up, I
tell them everything is being taken care of. But truthfully,

if we don't have at least a few minutes' warning, we're bound to have casualties. We're gambling with these people's lives.''

"We've substituted Justice Department employees wherever we can,'' Brognola said, "but we've had to hire some outsiders with creative potential to keep this company going. Here at Elwood we have a chance of stopping the terrorists. We have no chance of stopping them if they strike a new target.''

"But...." Ti began.

She was interrupted by the beeping of a pager that she wore on the belt of her jeans.

"The computer has monitored some activity on the central WAR computer,'' she said. "Shall we check it out now?''

"Might as well.''

When Lao Ti did not have a portable computer, she breadboarded her own. Miscellaneous boards of chips and a riot of wires filled an entire workbench. The only items Brognola recognized were a monitor, a keyboard and a bank of floppy-disk drives.

"Wouldn't this be better pulled together in a cabinet?'' he asked.

Ti shook her head. "Not at the rate I've got the clock set. Too much heat. If I really get going, I turn some fans on the bench to move the air faster.''

She sat down at the keyboard. Her fingers would blur for a few seconds and then pause while the screen filled with a mishmash of symbols. She would take these in at a glance and then her fingers would start their frantic dance once again.

The messages on the screen were as impossible to follow as the arcane symbols that Ti was entering. Often there was nothing but long strips of ones and zeros.

"Do either of you speak English?'' Brognola cracked.

Ti finished her high-speed rattling of the keyboard and then turned to Brognola with a smile.

"As a matter of fact, we both do, but not to each other. Machine language is more efficient.''

"I don't recognize any of the standard programming languages on that screen."

Ti shook her head. "Not programming language. Too slow. Machine language, the language the computer regulates itself with. Machine language is both stronger and faster."

"I'll buy that it's faster. What's happening?"

"Just let me finish and the three of us will start speaking English."

She scanned the screen and her fingers danced again. In another minute she had exchanged two more screens full of information with the computer. She then paused and thought for a moment, before starting back on the keyboard.

"I've separated out the everyday transactions from the ones we're interested in," she said. "Can Aaron join us? I think we'll need his help."

Brognola went to the lab next door. There, Aaron "The Bear" Kurtzman was at a more conventional computer terminal, directing the daily running of Elwood Electronic Industries. Brognola had insisted that Kurtzman join him in Atlanta. He knew the Bear was going stir-crazy in his new job at Stony Man Farm.

"You know, Hal, running a company can be fun," the big man said. "I think I'll take over some company when I retire."

"That'll take a fair-sized investment."

Kurtzman looked at Brognola and shook his head.

"Oh, no. I'll just use a computer like this and take over a company. They'll never quite figure out how it all happened."

"Before you get your hand too deep in the till, Ti says we need your help next door."

When they returned to Ti's lab, she had a bunch of pseudo words on the screen. She continued to study them while Kurtzman maneuvered his chair to where he could also see the screen.

"You recognize anything?" she asked, without looking up.

"Where'd you get that stuff?" Kurtzman demanded. His usually soft voice was gruff.

"Entry codes used recently by someone on the WAR computer. This computer is monitoring theirs."

"Those codes reach all sorts of information, both restricted and classified."

Ti pushed her chair back from the workbench.

"You better take over. I may trip one of the safety devices. We need to go in there and find what WAR got from those computers. Whoever did it was shrewd enough not to store anything. I have a record of the stuff sent, but it would take ages to go through everything in the order they did it."

Kurtzman's hands moved over the keys. His eyes stayed on the screen. He never looked down to see what his hands were doing.

"Damn," he spat after minutes of work.

"Damn," Ti repeated.

They both sat looking glumly at the screen.

"The damn terrorists must have found the government access codes at one of the places they wiped out," the Bear told Brognola. "They've dug into the federal computers and gone straight for any grant money awarded that's blanketed by security. They now know where every research establishment that is important to the government is, and what they're working on."

"Crap," Brognola fired. "I want a map with the location of every office and branch that WAR has and all the research that's going on within a thirty-mile radius of each branch."

"You realize that their offices are near Silicon Valley, Bionic Valley, Route 128 and all the big research centres?" Kurtzman asked. "You're talking about over half the computer research that's happening in the U.S."

"If it's that big a job, you'd better get moving," Brognola growled.

"Aaron," Ti said, "if you start pulling out names and addresses on your computer, I'll raid civil defense for computerized city maps. Then you batch your information over here, and I'll have my computer mark the locations on the maps. Give me an importance rating of one to five. We'll assign them colors. When we're through, we can batch the information onto the company computer and have the plotter print it six-color on eleven-by-seventeen paper.''

"You got it," the Bear told her.

July 13, 930 hours, Atlanta, Georgia

"WHERE ARE LOUIS, Rodrigos and Lobo?" Jishin demanded.

Lyons and Devine had not been summoned to report until the following morning. They stood facing her in the deserted recreation lounge.

"Who?" Lyons asked.

Jishin stared at Deborah, who raised her eyebrows. "Aren't they here?"

"No. They're not here. Yesterday they were sent to keep you two out of trouble. They haven't returned."

"Were they driving a beat-up pickup truck?" Lyons asked.

"Louis owns such a vehicle."

"We saw a beat-up truck following us when we were changing buses downtown. We didn't know who it was, so we ditched it," Lyons told the Japanese terrorist.

"Did you check the police and hospitals?" Deborah asked.

Jishin filled her lungs to say something and then let the breath back out again, slowly. "So what do our intelligence experts have to report?"

"Dr. Lao is just finishing a week off. She's due back at Elwood next week," Lyons reported, using the story that he and Deborah had carefully concocted.

"How did you manage to find this out?" Jishin's voice quavered with suspicion.

Lyons flashed the wallet he had stolen.

"We went in there as building inspector and assistant.

Looked the place over. Asked questions about an empty lab and got lucky with the answers.''

"You seem to have an extraordinary amount of skill and background in these matters," Jishin commented.

"Never been caught yet," Lyons answered. He gave Jishin a broad wink. Her face remained expressionless, but there was no question that she could barely tolerate big-mouthed Carl Leggit.

"I think you two might have done a good job. If so, there'll be a bonus and you'll be made team leaders for the raid. I'm not passing final judgment until I hear from the three who were supposed to protect you.

"In the meantime, you'll stay in this building until the time of the raid. I'll be in Boston, but I'm leaving instructions with Jim Saint to shoot anyone who leaves this building without direct orders. He's commander in my absence. Is all that quite clear?"

When Jishin left the room, Lyons turned to Deborah and leered.

"If we're going to be confined to quarters, we may as well enjoy it," he said. His voice was loud.

He grabbed Deborah by the hand and almost dragged her to the men's bunk room. There was only one occupant. The rest were in classes.

Lyons pushed her toward his bunk and went to the other occupant of the room.

"Ten bucks if you get out and watch the door for fifteen minutes," he whispered in the man's ear.

The guy glanced at Deborah. "Only fifteen minutes, huh? Who are you fooling?"

"C'mon, you know we'll be missed if we stay longer."

The guy pocketed the money and left, a silly leer plastered on his face.

Lyons went over to another bunk and turned on a radio. Then he beckoned Deborah. She came into his arms.

He whispered in her ear. "I don't know if the place is bugged or not. I've got to get to a telephone with that Boston bit. You stay here and cover for me."

"Okay," she whispered.

Lyons went to one of the two windows in the room. It was fitted with heavy mesh, bolted to the window frame.

He propped the window open, stood back and aimed a series of front kicks at the lower corners of the mesh. Three minutes later, the bolts had been dragged right through the wood frame. Lyons forced his way out between the window ledge and the bottom of the screen.

Deborah went over to the window and examined the screen. The kicks had been well placed and had done little damage to the mesh itself. She pulled the screen back into place. Then she put some pennies on the sill and closed the window. Lyons would be able to put his fingers underneath to raise the window again. Deborah had an uneasy feeling, a feeling of doom. She wanted Lyons's tracks covered as well as possible.

She was looking around for something to read when she heard angry voices in the hall. She quickly climbed into a bunk and covered up with her back to the door.

A moment later the door opened.

"For Christ's sake, get out!" Deborah cried without looking around.

Heavy boots crossed the floor and the covers were yanked off the bunk.

"Making love to yourself?" asked James Saint, his voice heavily laced with both an Irish brogue and venomous sarcasm.

"Just trying to get fifteen minutes to myself," Deborah answered. Her voice sounded weary.

"Where's Leggit?"

"How the hell should I know."

Deborah swung around and sat up. Saint stood towering over her. His blue eyes surveyed her coldly as he stood with his hands on his hips.

"Jones said he was in here with you."

Deborah stood up so suddenly she almost knocked Saint off his feet. He had to take a rapid step back to keep his balance.

"Where does this harassment stop?" she yelled. "First, you match me up with the boor in exercise class. Then you send me out for a day on the town with him. Some day! Now you expect me to sleep with the son-of-a-bitch. Go to hell!''

Saint was taken aback by the sudden onslaught. He looked at Deborah as if she had just sprouted horns and a tail. He went once around the room and looked in the washroom, but he found no one. He stopped in front of each of the two windows, but seemed satisfied that they were intact. His circuit of the room brought him back in front of Devine.

"Where's Leggit?" The voice was determined.

Deborah shrugged. "I haven't seen him since he got Jones out of here and let me have his bunk. He and Jones left together.''

"What's wrong with your own bunk?"

"The place is full of yappy females.''

He slapped her hard enough to rock her on her feet. She bent her knees and went with the blow. Only her karate training enabled her to keep her feet.

"You're lying."

She launched a body blow that hit the hard-muscled stomach with enough force that Saint had to take a step backward. He backed up one more step and produced an American Arms TP-70 from his trouser side pocket. The little .25 caliber automatic stared like death into Deborah's face.

"You do *not* strike a superior officer," Saint grated. "You'll be disciplined for this, but first I'm going to find Leggit.''

The automatic gestured toward the door. "Out.''

"I demand to see Aya Jishin.''

"Tough shit, Devine. Jishin just left. I'm in charge. Now move.''

"Where to?''

"The brig. You stay there until we get this thing sorted out.''

Deborah turned to hide a shudder. The brig was a cage in the basement. It was used for punishment. A person could neither stand, sit, nor lie straight in the brig. Things were falling apart in a hell of a hurry. She pulled her shoulders straight and marched out of the room.

July 13, 951 hours, Smyrna, Georgia

"EXACTLY WHAT DID CARL SAY?" Politician asked.

Pol, Gadgets, the Bear and Ti were sitting in front of Brognola's desk at Elwood Electronic Industries. Behind the desk Brognola sat very straight, his forehead creased with worry lines.

"Not much," he answered. "He'd slipped out of the building and was worried about being missed. All he knew was that Jishin let it slip she was leaving for Boston right away. He has a hunch that a raid is imminent in that area."

"We might be able to get military transport and arrive the same time she does, but there's no way to beat her there," Gadgets pointed out.

"No idea how long we have?" Pol probed.

Brognola shook his head.

"Is there anyone left at Stony Man?" Gadgets asked. "If so, they can get to Boston a lot faster than we can."

Brognola nodded. "Phoenix Force's Manning and McCarter are watching the shop. They can be in Boston in a matter of minutes."

"Okay, Manning and McCarter can get to Boston on time, but what's the target?" Gadgets wondered aloud.

Kurtzman spoke for the first time. "I think we can answer that one. Ti and I have been assembling maps of probable targets within striking distance of WAR's main branches. The Boston area has one target that's several times as important as any other in the area—MIT."

"What's so special about the Massachusetts Institute of Technology?" Brognola asked.

"They've assembled some of the most promising younger researchers. A lot of federal funds have gone there recently to back several hush-hush computer projects. And a university is always an easy target. I'd say it's MIT with a ninety-six-percent probability."

"That's close enough," Brognola decided. He reached for the telephone to call Stony Man. "I just hope we manage things on time. One of you get me Quantico Marine Base on the other line."

12

The captain was in a cranky mood. He had been off duty and just about to sit down to enjoy a couple of drinks in the officers' mess, when the officer of the day had caught him.

"Jackson. Top-priority flight, on the double."

"Hey, Colonel. I'm not on the duty roster."

"You are now. Jump."

Captain Jackson got the message. He got to the chopper hangar on the double—it was on the double all the way, because Colonel Fulton jogged right beside him.

They came to a stop beside a Sikorsky CH-53E. It was already warming up. The captain reached for the clipboard being held by a mechanic, but Fulton snatched it and scribbled a quick signature without checking it. Jackson was beginning to suspect that the flight was more than routine.

"Where's my crew?" he asked.

"You're the crew," Fulton told him as they boarded. "I'm commanding."

"But you're duty officer."

"And duty calls."

They warmed up the sixteen-ton helicopter and staggered it into the sky the moment the engines would take it.

"Where's the load, skipper?" Jackson asked. He was beginning to feel the excitement.

"Just outside the Shenandoah Park. There's two passengers for Boston."

"We're taking this gas-guzzling, suicidal monster to ferry two men?"

The colonel was enjoying the captain's discomfort. "It's

the fastest thing we've got on the base, and I was told it had to be the quickest merry-go-round we have.''

''Who gave that brilliant order?''

''Not allowed to say, but it came from a lot higher than base commander.''

The lights around the helipad were strongly directional. Jackson did not spot them until they were directly over them. The colonel brought the chopper back on a much lower level and then down on the pad. The lights went out immediately. Jackson cranked the door and jumped out.

For all he knew he might be in the middle of a meadow. He wondered how grass could be used without showing signs of wear. He bent down and discovered he was standing on Astro Turf.

Two men in camouflage fatigues came jogging up with a war bag in each of their hands. They moved swiftly and easily. Jackson wondered what they could be carrying that would be that bulky, that light and that important.

The two men looked like brothers. They were both slightly under six feet, both muscular, but their facial features were different. It was obvious they were both fighting men.

''Rough air ahead. I'll store those,'' Jackson told the passengers.

''Like hell you will, mate,'' said the one with longer hair. Then, with a flash of the devil in his blue eyes, he added, ''But you could give me a bloody hand getting this crap aboard.''

He extended the two war bags at arm's length to the curious marine captain. Jackson reached forward, took the straps and then staggered forward. His arms dropped and the bags swung into his legs with a dull clunk. It was all Jackson could do to hold on to the bags and not moan out loud. Each bag weighed about seventy pounds.

The other passenger placed both of his bags on the helicopter, and without removing his hands from their grip, vaulted on after them. The one with the British accent easily clambered aboard and accepted his war bags from Jackson. Jackson had to lift them one at a time.

"Don't know what I'd have done without you," the passenger told him.

Jackson looked into the mocking blue eyes and canceled his scowl. He dogged the door and hurried to the flight deck.

"Let's get out of here, sir," he told the colonel.

"What are our passengers like?" Fulton asked as he slapped the Sikorsky into maximum climb.

The acceleration pushed Jackson into his seat before he was buckled in.

"I met someone like those two once before," Jackson said. "A big dark guy with icy eyes."

Jackson paused and shuddered.

"Colonel, the rpm are red zone."

"Them's our orders. This chopper only has to last long enough to get them to MIT."

"There's no pad at MIT."

"That's what I told them," Fulton said.

"And what was the response?" the captain asked.

Colonel Fulton grinned. "Tough," he quoted.

July 13, 1148 hours, Cambridge, Massachusetts

AYA JISHIN STOOD at the front of the bus and looked down its length, assessing what she saw. She had twenty of her Cambodia- and Moscow-trained specialists with her. The other thirty passengers were locals, recruited and trained through HIT. The specialists all sat at the front, near her. It would not do for them to mingle with the foot soldiers.

The bus gave a sudden swerve. She fired an angry glare at the driver. He was wiping a hand on his pants and paying little attention to the road.

He caught the glance and explained uneasily. "Whoever slit the driver's throat got blood on the controls. It's getting sticky."

"Be thankful it isn't your blood," Jishin told him.

The driver looked straight ahead and did not answer. He was noticeably paler.

Jishin was genuinely annoyed with him. What was a little blood? Did they expect to destroy a system without getting blood on their hands? Americans isolated themselves from reality to an extent her Japanese mind could never fathom. There had been only six passengers on the bus, all older people. If there had been forty-odd women and children, she doubted if these troops would have even seized the bus.

They pulled onto the campus of MIT. Harvard was right next door along the Charles River.

"Which building do we want?" the driver asked.

Jishin pulled out a crumpled campus guide and shoved it at the driver. One of the buildings was circled.

"Not many people around for this time of day," someone observed.

"We're being flagged down," the driver said.

A workman in beige coveralls was in front of the bus, madly waving a red flag.

"Stop and see what he wants," Jishin ordered.

Her internal alarms were buzzing. The campus was too quiet for midmorning.

The driver stopped and opened the doors of the bus. The workman, a rugged blond-haired man, bounced on board as if he wanted to fight. His attitude lulled Jishin's suspicions slightly. People who lay ambushes try not to look overly aggressive.

"You idiot. Don't you know you're driving into a blast zone?" the worker demanded.

"Blast zone?" The driver was genuinely perplexed.

"Like they told you at the gate—no one on campus until the blast is set off."

"What blast?" The driver was almost whining.

Jishin was almost convinced, until she locked eyes with the man. His face was surprisingly controlled for a longnose, but he could not totally hide the recognition that flashed behind his eyes. He raised his yellow hard hat to the Japanese terrorist.

"The blast that's just about to happen," he told the driver. Then he leaped off the bus.

Attention was distracted by the smashing of the rear

window of the bus. The glass fell inward on the American terrorists-in-training, followed by two hand grenades.

Jishin forgot all about the workman and threw herself into the laps of two terrorists in the front seat. She yelled, "Grenade!" while she was in the air.

The blasts made mincemeat of much of the local talent, but did nothing to the professionals at the front of the bus. Being thoroughly trained professionals, they held their seats while the survivors from the back of the bus pushed and shoved in their desperate haste to get off the rolling death trap.

Jishin regained her feet and barked commands. "Weapons out and look sharp. Throw yourselves flat and return any fire. Don't push each other, push that smart ass out there."

Her hoarse, drill-sergeant voice brought them short. It was evident that they still had more fear of Jishin than they had of grenades. M-16s were readied and cocked. The trainees left the bus and hit the close-cropped lawn like trained infantry. They spread and started to return the machine-gun fire that cut into them from the corner of a nearby building.

The driver started to leave his seat. Jishin pushed him back roughly.

"Fool! Don't you go running out into an ambush. Get this thing out of here."

The driver took no more convincing. The bus took off, careening around the orderly but deserted drives, heading for Cambridge traffic. On board were Jishin, twenty Communist-trained terrorists, seven dead terrorists-in-training and three who were so wounded that they had been unable to leave the bus. The professionals used knives to silence those three as they sped from ambush.

July 13, 1002 hours, Atlanta, Georgia

LYONS HAD HAD TO JOG almost two miles before finding a telephone. His return to the window was cautious.

He noticed that the window was down. He walked up to

it slowly. Four terrorists rushed him. Lyons caught the motion out of the corner of his eye.

The first thug to reach him came from the left. He ran straight into a spear hand to the larynx. The terrorist lay down and drowned in his own blood.

Lyons side kicked the idiot diving at him from the right. The man's low flight took him straight into the whipping boot. A loud snap sounded as the man's neck broke.

The impact put the Able Team warrior slightly off balance, causing him to spin ninety degrees before he could put his foot down and brace himself. By that time, the last two were on top of him—one wore brass knuckles, the other had a small blackjack. Lyons jerked his head to one side. The brass knuckles painfully scraped one ear.

Lyons backed up quickly, trying to separate himself from the attackers. The goon with the brass knuckles attacked. His flurry of blows bruised Lyons's forearms and opened a cut on his cheek. Lyons suddenly lashed out with his foot. The fighter with the knuckles coolly twisted and took the kick on the thigh, lashing out with a jab as he did so.

The scrappy blond deflected the jab with a punch to the forearm. He then saw that the other terrorist was circling to come at him from behind. Before the man could move in behind him, he launched a swift assault against the animal with the knuckles. He advanced with a series of kicks. His enemy managed to dodge one and deflect one, but a third kick crashed into open ribs, sending the goon staggering.

Lyons whirled on the blackjack wielder just in time to drive his knuckles into the back of the hand wielding the weapon. The goon tried to score with a backswing, but had his hand hit again. A shout of agony escaped his lips, but he hung onto the sap.

Lyons then stepped to one side and spun around. His other opponent nearly bowled his ally off his feet as he charged right past where Lyons had been. Carl hurried the charge with a boot to the calf.

Both men swung to face him. This time they were both

on the same side of their intended victim. Lyons rapidly closed in on the terrorist with the brass knuckles, giving him no time to get set or to think. He intercepted a straight jab by grabbing the wrist with his right hand and locking the elbow with his left. He gave a hard pull, levering one opponent into the other. The moment the two thugs collided, they lost the match.

Lyons was instantly upon them. He dropped the terrorist with the brass knuckles with a short, sharp kidney punch. The killer with the blackjack received a foot stomp that ended his useless life. The other left the world after taking a blow to the temple.

Lyons walked around the building until he found where the power cables entered. His job was clear cut—get Deborah away from about forty armed terrorists and do it before they could react and kill her.

He pulled the Colt Python from the holster in the small of his back. It was not his usual gun. He had chosen a simple four-inch barrel, .357 Magnum. He could not spare the pocket space for rapid loaders. The bulk would have shown, but he did have extra ammunition distributed around his pockets, about twenty extra rounds. It was not much, but it had to be enough.

He fired two 200-grain bullets into the power transformer that served the building. While the transformer arced and died, he replaced the two spent shells with live rounds. He then walked to the front of the building.

The front quarter of the ground floor was just that—a front. Step two was to remove these naive types from the battle zone.

Lyons put a hand to his cheek. It was still oozing blood. He wiped the hand clean, first on his forehead and then on his shirtfront. By that time he was passing the large display window in the front of the building.

The WAR volunteer workers were bustling around because the electric typewriters and the copier no longer worked. They stopped bustling and stared when a blood-smeared monstrosity kicked in the display window and strode over the broken glass, gun in hand.

The only person in the office who was not suddenly frozen was a redheaded secretary outside the manager's office. She produced a .25 Bauer automatic with her right hand, while reaching for a concealed buzzer with her left. A single, lead mind stopper canceled the intentions of both hands.

"You have thirty seconds to get out of here," Lyons shouted.

All took the hint.

Lyons went through the empty manager's office to the door in back. He knew his first stop had to be the firing range in the basement. There he could arm himself and cut off the access to the guns and supplies of ammunition. The brig or cage was not far from the range. That would be the next step. He figured that would be where they had put Deborah.

He reached the stairs to the basement without incident. However, James Saint and two of the imported terrorists came out of the firing range just as he reached the bottom of the steps. Saint was not slow. His first glance at the gun-toting, blood-smeared apparition was sufficient.

"Get him," Saint commanded.

Saint backed his command with a flying dive through the door to the firing range. His two henchmen did not have guns in their hands; Lyons did. The two terrorists never had guns in their hands again. The first was still trying to get a hand under his shirt when the 200-grain Magnum went through the hand, through the shirt and through the terrorist, removing three inches of spine from his back.

The second killer managed to produce an ancient Astra 400 from his side pocket before a bullet made mush out of his face.

Lyons scooped up the unfired Astra. He hoped the 1921 model automatic would not blow up in his hand, but he needed every shot he could find. Before following Saint into the firing range, he paused to recharge the Colt.

Before he could continue, he heard Deborah Devine shout. "Carl. Not in here. It's a trap." Then she screamed. The voice came from the brig area of the basement.

At the bottom of the steps there was a small hall off which opened three doors. One went to a storage cupboard and was always locked. Another was for the firing range and the third was for a utility room, which contained the cage.

"I heard you. Thanks," Lyons called out.

Then he hit the door.

The ruse had worked.

Six of the hard-core terrorists were in the room with the cage. They all had M-16s. When Lyons called that he had the message, they went into motion to pursue him. When the door swung inward, it caught one terror goon in the face. The other five were all in motion and not set. They never had a chance to get set.

Lyons fired both the revolver and the automatic, one from each hand—twelve bullets. Each ambusher had his ticket to hell punched twice.

Deborah was curled in the cage. Her clothing was torn and there were some cigarette burns on her back and buttocks.

"God, am I glad to see you," she gushed.

Lyons just nodded as he charged the Colt once more. He put it back in its concealed holster and then released her. While he tended to the guns, Deborah did a quick-change act. She peeled her torn clothing and took pants and shirt from the body that was closest to her size. It was a common-sense action, done quickly and efficiently.

Lyons's eyes reflected a rare warmth when he handed her two of the M-16s. In return, she gave him a smile—shaky, but genuine.

"What's next, boss?"

"Next, we close this joint down."

There was no argument, no discussion of the odds, no mention of referring the decision up the chain of command. She merely nodded, checked the clips on both rifles and waited for further instructions.

"A large group are holed up in the firing range, waiting for us," Lyons told Devine. "We can't attack and we can't get out of here past them."

"So?"

"So find some black tape on the workbench."

While Deborah sifted through the clutter on the workbench, Lyons got two cans of Coke from one of the coin machines.

"No tape, but there's some black spray paint."

"It will have to do. Blacken these as fast as possible."

He tossed her the cans of Coke.

"Just the right size for Israeli grenades," she commented.

"Let's hope they think so."

Deborah was back within a minute. The cans dripped paint across the floor and down her left hand. Both fighters held their cocked automatic rifles ready to fire with one hand.

Lyons took a slippery can of pop in his left hand and put half a clip of .223s through the opposite door.

It took only five paces to cross the hall and kick the door to the firing range open the rest of the way. Both fighters launched their blackened cans of pop through the door, paused one second and followed.

There was a strangled cry. "Hand bomb!"

When the warriors stepped into the room, every killer's eye was still fastened on the soaring cans of Coke.

Deborah emptied one M-16 in a sweeping motion that cut across every standing terrorist in the room. She then ducked behind a gun cabinet and started to pick at individuals.

Lyons fired short bursts, taking out Saint and the terror goons he felt most dangerous. He used the half clip and then a full clip with lightning-fast selective shooting.

The battle of the firing range was over before most of the participants were aware that it had begun. Devine and Lyons looked at each other and then at the clutter of bodies. There were ten goons who would never again kill a computer scientist. Lyons opened a cabinet and lifted out a batch of clips for the M-16s.

When they left the firing range, Deborah carried three loaded autorifles. Lyons carried six, five of which were slung on his right shoulder.

Two curious faces looked down the steps to the basement. Both faces vanished in a spray of red. The sound of weapons' fire outside the firing range brought one student to the door of the dojo. Lyons saw him and waved him over. The curious student came over and received a single shot through the eye. At the same time, Deborah stepped through the doorway to the karate-training gym and took out the rest of the class.

The mop up was quick, brutal. No one was left in the terrorist wing of the WAR building. By the time it was finished, the sound of a siren was near. Someone from the front part had telephoned the police. Lyons and Deborah dropped the M-16s and left the building by a fire exit.

13

July 13, 1313 hours, Smyrna, Georgia

Hal Brognola was in the chief executive's office at Elwood Electronic Industries, talking on the telephone. Whatever the conversation was about, he did not appear pleased. In his ashtray were the remains of his last cigar. It had been bitten in two. When Lyons and Deborah appeared in the doorway, his frown deepened.

Lyons flopped into a chair and indicated one for Deborah.

"How many got away?" Brognola said into the phone. "How the hell did they get booked onto flights so fast? Shit!" Brognola paused and thought for about five seconds. "I'll have to call back. Carl's just come in and has something to report. Give me a telephone number. Okay. I've got that. Stand by."

Brognola hung up the telephone. He again picked up the receiver and dialed a number inside the company.

"Ti, can you get in here right away. Carl's just come in and things have gone sour in Boston. On second thought, find some chairs and coffee, we'll come to you. We're probably going to have to include your computer in this conference."

He hung up without waiting for an answer and dialed another three-digit number.

"Aaron, Ti's lab as quickly as you can make it. Find Pol and Gadgets. They're somewhere in the building. Bring them along."

Brognola pushed his chair back and stood up, but made no move toward the door. "Perhaps you'd better reintroduce us," he told Lyons.

"Hal, this is Deborah Devine, state cop. Deborah, this is Hal Brognola, head Fed."

Deborah gave Brognola a firm handshake.

Brognola headed for the door. "Come on," he said over his shoulder. "I want to hear what happened, but you might as well tell it to everybody at once."

When they filed into Ti's lab, the Bear, Pol and Gadgets were already there.

Ti looked furious. "Mr. Brognola," she said formally, "you hung up on me before I could give my report—I also have bad news."

Brognola just shook his head. "Report," he sighed.

"About twenty minutes ago, there was a long-distance collect call from Boston to the computer center in Santa Clara. The computer recorded it. I was listening to it when you called. Now, there has been a sudden burst of computer activity. They're using the interface with the smaller computers in their major cities to send the messages."

Brognola held up his hand to stop Ti at that point. "Let me tell everyone what happened in Boston. Then the rest of your report will make more sense."

Ti nodded.

"You and your computer had already determined that Jishin's most probable target was the Massachusetts Institute of Technology, the lab where they're doing work on supercooled, superspeed computers. We rushed Manning and McCarter there just in case. They set up an ambush and sprang it as soon as they made a positive identification of the terrorists. Unfortunately Jishin was able to sacrifice her homegrown terrorists and get away with the hard-core international killers, ones that were Moscow trained.

"They had already wiped out the driver and six passengers when they commandeered a bus. They used the bus to drive back to Logan International Airport. There they simply killed passengers for their tickets and bookings and climbed onto domestic flights where they wouldn't have to show identification. That left twenty-two more bodies at the airport. Manning and McCarter are having the destinations of the victims checked out, and are standing by for further instructions."

Ti did not give them time to discuss the tragedy in Boston. Her fingers flew over the computer keyboard. Suddenly Jishin's hoarse voice rasped from a speaker.

"This is Commander Jishin. I wish orders sent out to all branches immediately."

"Yes, Commander."

"Condition red. All base commanders are to destroy their targets tomorrow at twelve hundred hours. Have you got that?"

"Yes, Commander."

"Then send it immediately. I'll call in a few hours for acknowledgments."

The line went dead. Over the dial tone, the man in Santa Clara said, "Yes, Commander."

The group sat in silence. Brognola stood up. "I have a telephone call to make. Everyone please wait for a couple of minutes." Then he strode out of the lab.

By the time Lyons had introduced Deborah to the rest of the Stony Man crew, Brognola was back. He sat behind the desk and sighed.

"It's up to us," he announced. "As I said at the top of this mission, this is an election year. The President will not use the army, the FBI nor the Justice Department against HIT. He seems worried that it'll appear that he's attacking the unemployed."

"Politics," Gadgets spat. He said it as a dirty word.

No one else said a thing.

"So we have only ourselves and a strike planned from each of the HIT training centers," Brognola said. His voice was heavy.

"Not quite," Ti corrected. "Our computer is holding the command. It hasn't passed it on to the branches yet. I thought we might just not pass it along, but give phony acknowledgments."

"Do you know the acknowledgment routine?" Brognola asked.

Ti shook her head.

"Then let's pass the command along but stagger the orders, One city every two days. That will give us time to cope."

Deborah spoke up. "It won't work. There's a daily log. The change in orders will be discovered by five o'clock tonight."

"Let's figure the minimum time spread we need," Gadgets said. "We'll send the first order to strike on schedule and spread the rest. That will give us some acknowledgments. We can use those to fake the rest."

"What cities do we have to cover?" Brognola asked Ti.

"Atlanta, Boston, Houston, Kansas City, Los Angeles, Minneapolis, Salt Lake City and Seattle."

"All those. Start by eliminating Boston. We're standing by there already."

Ti's fingers flew over the keys. "Done," she reported.

"I think we'd better get Yakov to Seattle right away," Pol suggested. "He's the only one close enough to do anything if we don't manage a decent delay."

Brognola turned to Kurtzman. "Run me a package of all the information we have on the Seattle branch of HIT. I'll give it to Yakov as soon as I can get him to the telephone.

"The rest of you work out a schedule for covering these various branches. We can't afford to lose more computer people."

Brognola picked up a telephone and began the tedious process of placing a secure call to the head of Phoenix Force, who was a guest of the Canadian government at an antiterrorist conference somewhere in or near Vancouver.

Kurtzman wheeled up to the desk with a few sheets of printout before the call was through. The call took nineteen minutes to place and six minutes to transact, including relaying all the information that Kurtzman had summed up.

Brognola hung up the telephone, then spent another six minutes arranging arms and transportation for the Israeli terror fighter. When he was finished, he leaned back and looked at his team.

"What have you come up with?"

"First, while you were on the telephone, the acknowl-edgment came back from Boston," Ti said. "It was nega-tive. Apparently the Boston commander feels that he's already lost all those with enough training to conduct a raid."

"I'm in favor of letting the message go through and see-ing what the reaction is," Brognola said.

"Can't hurt," Politician said.

Ti picked up the report on the group discussion. "We can rule out an attack here in Atlanta. There's no one to do it. We think the command should go through to sit in the untended computer in case Jishin returns."

Politician took up the report while Ti worked. "The next most difficult place for us to reach in decent time is Minneapolis. My guess is that some of those professional terrorists are going to each destination to back up the local HIT teams.

"Gadgets and I have a business there. My sister, Toni, runs it. We suggest that you arrange for the FBI to take Toni along and meet the next couple of flights from Boston. The idea is to try to find a reason to hold the ter-rorists and prevent them from beefing up the locals. If we schedule things correctly, Gadgets, Carl and I can take care of Kansas City and have Jack fly us to Minneapolis, and later, on to Salt Lake City. If we put a four-or-five-hour time differential in their attack orders, we should be able to handle all three cities ourselves."

"Besides," Gadgets added, "we'll have Toni keeping an eye on things in case they break wrong."

"Sounds okay," Brognola agreed. "I could get the FBI to help on a watchdog basis—as long as they weren't in-volved in the actual fighting. That leaves Texas and California. I can reach Texas easily enough, but California is a long way away."

"So you go straight there by military jet," Pol said. "We'll schedule it about last to give you the most time. Babette can keep an eye on the activity in their office in Santa Clara and alert you if something goes off schedule."

"What about Houston?"

"We thought you could bring Manning and McCarter down from Boston. That will leave Stony Man without a temporary commander. We suggest that Aaron get there as quickly as possible to coordinate all our activities," Ti said.

"What about keeping this place running?" Brognola asked.

"Deborah and I will just have to manage somehow. With the Atlanta office wiped out, it's unlikely we'll have an attack to deal with. I'll stay in touch with Aaron and help with the coordination."

Brognola thought for a few seconds before deciding. "With only ourselves to rely on, you've come up with the most workable plan. Get those messages out and let's go to work. I just hope we can—"

He was interrupted by the telephone. He scooped it up and growled, "Brognola." Then he sat and listened.

"Good work," he said, finally. "Stay at the airport. I'm arranging for you to be flown to Houston to stop a raid there. Stand by, Kurtzman will give you the intel."

The Bear wheeled over to the computer terminal, taking the telephone with him.

Brognola updated the rest of the group.

"Your analysis is depressingly correct. By identifying most of the bodies and finding out where they were booked to fly, we know that professional terrorists are on their way to Minneapolis-St. Paul, Los Angeles, Houston, Salt Lake City, Kansas City and Seattle."

July 13, 1602 hours, St. Paul, Minnesota

FBI AGENT TIM WILLIAMS LOOKED at his partner Carlos Sanchez. Sanchez shrugged. Neither of them liked the assignment, but orders were orders. They would delay the flights from Boston and try to question the passengers. That was routine, but why was a civilian keeping an eye on them? A licensed private detective at that. It was degrading.

Williams glanced at the detective. Not hard to glance at.

She was a small woman. She looked as though she was in her early twenties, but there was a poise, a sense of experience. She wore her hair long, and brushed until it gleamed. The makeup was subtle. It could afford to be; she had big dark eyes that could drive a man wild. A good figure, too. Williams tore his eyes away to get his mind back to the unpleasant assignment.

"Miss Blancanales," Sanchez said to the woman.

"Friends call me Toni," she said.

"Miss Blancanales," Sanchez continued, "we can't stop every passenger from these flights and say 'Are you a terrorist?' What do you expect us to do?"

"Well, Mr. Sanchez, you might pay special attention to anyone who doesn't wait for his or her luggage, or who has to read tag numbers in order to identify it," Toni said.

Williams reflected that it was a solid suggestion. If the terrorists killed for the airline tickets and bookings, they would have no use for any luggage that was checked. He hastened to agree with the woman and save Sanchez from having to do so.

"A good suggestion, Miss Blancanales. We'll do that."

"Thank you," she answered. Then she spun on her heels and walked away, later standing far enough from the agents not to be associated with them, but close enough to observe. The location was not lost on Sanchez.

"Fink dame," he muttered under his breath.

There was no more time to simmer. The flight they wanted was in and the first passengers were trickling into the terminal building. Of the first half dozen, two men and a woman headed straight for the exit. With an uneasy glance at Toni Blancanales, the two FBI men moved to intercept the three.

All three were calm. Too calm. Each asked if they were under arrest. Each insisted that they had an important appointment and could not be delayed. Finally, each insisted that they be charged or released. Williams glanced at Sanchez.

"Do we hold them?" Williams asked.

"On what grounds?"

"Come off it, Sanchez. You know we can always dream up a reason. These three are too smooth for my taste."

Sanchez shrugged. "Let's lay it on the queen and let her decide." He glanced at where the female detective had been watching. She was no longer there. "Hell, she doesn't even care enough to stick around. We've got no grounds to hold them."

Sanchez turned back to the three. "Go ahead," he told them. "Sorry to have had to delay you."

The trio hurried out of the terminal. Just as the doors closed behind them, Toni came from the other direction.

"I managed to look into the baggage that's supposed to belong to two of them," she told the FBI agent. "The clothing couldn't possibly fit."

Sanchez turned dull red. "You can't search baggage without a warrant," he bellowed at her.

People stopped to stare at them.

"For Christ's sake. Cool it," Williams warned his partner.

"Where are they?" Toni demanded.

"We had no reason to hold them. I let them go," Sanchez said in a lower tone of voice.

"You did what!"

"Listen, lady," Sanchez said, obviously deciding the best defense was an offense. "If you went into luggage without a warrant, I'm arresting you right now."

Toni ignored the threat. "You'll never find a witness," she told Sanchez. "My firm supplies the security here. When I read about innocent people being killed by those terrorists, I'll be thinking of you."

She turned and stalked away.

Sanchez watched her go, before leading the way to the agency car. He threw the keys to Williams, and then hunched himself low in the passenger seat.

"So will I," he muttered to himself. "So will I."

14

July 13, 1738 hours, Kansas City, Kansas

Carl Lyons watched the twelve men come out of the terminal building and divide into three taxis. The drivers stowed the heavy dunnage bags, two per cab, in the trunks and the cars pulled out in procession.

Lyons spoke into a microphone. "That's our boys. Let's follow them."

From a van farther along the road, Gadgets acknowledged. "We have them in our rearview mirror."

Lyons pulled his rented T-bird in behind the three cabs. He could see the van ahead, innocently leading the way. Pol would be driving, Gadgets keeping track of the quarry and the communications.

After a few miles the cavalcade turned into a doughnut-shop parking lot. Terrorists clambered out of all three taxis and went inside. Lyons saw the van pull over to the curb, three blocks ahead.

"Keep a parallel track," he told Gadgets over his radio. "If you stop and then pull back into the parade, they'll spot you for sure. It shouldn't be too hard. We know where they're headed."

"We know where we *think* they're headed," Gadgets answered.

"That'll have to do. Hold position until you see them start up. Then get out of sight. Something smells here. I'm going to go in."

Lyons pulled into the parking lot and went in. He noticed that only some of the terrorists were buying coffee and doughnuts. Those who were were getting them to go. One man was at the pay phone.

Lyons bought some doughnuts to go. About that moment, the guy on the telephone finished his call and headed for the door. Immediately the other eleven followed.

Lyons wandered back to his car and continued the pursuit. The base of his neck was tingling. He did not like that telephone call.

Lyons spoke into the microphone. "Gadgets?"

"Running one block south."

"Cut in the afterburners and get there fast. Got EVA two or three blocks away. I think one or both of us is being led down the garden path."

"We're gone."

Lyons slapped his jacket, checking the positioning of the big Python. It rode comfortably in the custom breakaway clip under his left arm. He then reached over the seat, dragged a large salesman's sample case into the front seat, and undid the catches.

At the next traffic light, he slipped on a bandolier filled with clips. He also had time to strap a thigh holster and Ingram to his left leg. The light changed and he hurried to close the gap with the three taxis. At one point he held the car straight while he jammed a clip into the Atchisson Assault shotgun. He levered a round into the chamber and set the piece back down within the case.

Ahead, the caravan had sped up. If Lyons's figured the map correctly, they were five minutes from the old, four-story department store that WAR used as a barracks and training center.

When the cars ahead picked up speed once more, Lyons knew he had been spotted for sure. He began to close the gap. Rush-hour traffic was starting to thin out and the Thunderbird was more maneuverable than the taxis. Lyons felt it was better to push them than let them get away too easily.

The cars turned into an alley that ran along the side of the HIT headquarters. Lyons turned in after them, hoping to use the car to bottle them in a dead end.

Just as he committed himself, Gadgets squawked over

the radio. "Don't go into the alley beside the building. It's a set."

Lyons jammed on the brakes and thumbed the radio button at the same time.

"Too late. I'm in."

"Try to make it into the building," Gadgets said as Lyons dropped the microphone.

Lyons grabbed the Atchisson and put it on full auto. He jumped from the car and raked the sky with a six-shot clip. The sky was suddenly filled with four hundred pieces of lead, all looking for someone to rip open. The snipers who were leaning over the edges of the building to strafe Lyons's car with their M-16s never got a chance to pull the trigger. Three were killed. Three were unhit, but had jerked back and were in no position to fire.

Lyons leaped to the top of the T-bird. From there he crashed headfirst through a second-floor window of the HIT headquarters.

Behind him, he heard the snipers firing too late at nothing at all. He found himself alone in a barracks room. He slapped a new clip into the Atchisson and headed for the door.

Lyons crouched low and swung the door open. Automatic fire raked the doorway. He tumbled back and waited, but no one charged.

There was suddenly the sound of firing somewhere else in the building—Pol and Gadgets were on their way. Lyons pulled a mattress from one of the bunks and tossed it out the door. It stopped about three clips worth of ammunition. The next mattress landed on top of the remains of the first. It attracted even less lead. The third mattress collected one short burst. The fourth and fifth landed on top of the pile undamaged.

Having lulled the enemy, Lyons thrust the Atchisson around the doorway and fired a three-round burst to one side. He was back, away from the opening before there was any return fire. When the firing died down, someone was still screaming.

The sixth mattress collected another sixty or seven

rounds of .223 ammo. Then heavy firing broke out to one side of the doorway as Gadgets and Pol arrived.

Lyons ignored the direction of the firing and dropped behind his thick wall of mattresses. The terror goons at the other end of the hall had begun a charge to help their fellow killers. They found themselves facing the end of the Atchisson.

While Pol and Gadgets mopped up one end of the hall, Lyons reasoned with the terrorists who were charging from the other end. The steady boom, boom, boom of the Atchisson demolished all arguments for terrorism.

"Where are the pros?" Lyons demanded as soon as the rest of Able Team joined him.

"Gone. They never stopped," Gadgets reported.

Lyons led the way down a side hall, opening doors as he went, but there seemed to be nobody left in the building. Suddenly Lyons stopped and listened.

"Sirens already, and we have a dozen killers running around and no idea where they are," he said over his shoulder.

"Not right," Pol corrected him. "While you stopped at the doughnut shop, Gadgets went back and put a beeper on one of the taxis just in case."

"Let's go," Lyons said, leading the way downstairs at a full run.

Pol drove the van while Gadgets used the radio. Lyons followed in the T-bird. Soon they were headed north.

"Looks as if we're headed back to the airport," Lyons said through the microphone.

"More likely Fairfax Municipal Airport this time," Gadgets replied. "It's on the other side of the river."

A little later Gadgets broadcast again. "The signal is coming back toward us."

Lyons sped the T-bird around the van. As soon as he spotted one of the taxis he had been following, he steered the Ford into the oncoming lanes and stopped it in front of the taxi. It took a few millimeters from the brake lining, but the driver managed to stop the cab on time.

He stuck his head out the window and yelled. "You nut! Get yourself wiped out by someone else."

Lyons walked up to the driver's window. Then he pulled a wad of money from his pocket. As the driver watched he peeled off a five and a twenty.

"Your fare from the airport, downtown and back here, where did you drop them?"

The driver stuck his hand out the window. Lyons put the money into it.

"Acme Charter Service. The orange building over there. They're as nuts as you are."

Lyons laughed and tossed another five into the cab before returning to his car.

"Not nearly as nuts as I am," he told the startled driver.

"Yeah. They chartered an executive jet to St. Paul. You'll never catch up to them," the clerk at the charter-flight office told them.

Lyons turned to Gadgets. "Get Grimaldi here. Now."

15

July 13, 2004 hours, Minneapolis, Minnesota

J. Courtney Cain was a man who loved to talk. Usually it was not necessary for others to be willing to talk; it was enough that they should simply listen. However, in this case, he wanted his prisoner to talk and found her refusal to do so very frustrating.

Cain mechanically slapped his swagger stick against his right leg as he stared at Toni Blancanales. The stick tapped against carefully pressed fatigues, which Cain thought made him look very military. Unfortunately, at five-foot two, with long hair combed back to cover a bald spot, he looked more comic than military, a deficiency he found difficult to ignore when he saw the mockery in his prisoner's dark eyes.

"I am not entirely stupid...." J. Courtney began.

He stopped when he noticed the quirk at the corner of Toni's lips. He regretted his choice of phrase. The swagger stick whistled, Toni's head was jerked to one side. Soon an angry welt began to form on one cheek, just under the right eye. It joined three similar welts on the left side of her face. She struggled briefly against the ropes that held her to a wooden chair. Then her head dropped.

Cain tried again. As he spoke he paced back and forth in front of Toni, waving his stick and speaking as if he were addressing a class.

"First, Atlanta gets pounded during a raid. They lose half their force. Then Boston gets mauled during a raid and the rest of Atlanta's HIT trainees get wiped.

"It doesn't take much brains to figure that there's some sort of a force after us. Now I'm told that our trainees have been massacred in Kansas. That leaves me with the distinctly uncomfortable feeling that we may be next, here in Minneapolis. So, you can see that I was already on the alert. And when I do a sweep of the area, what do I find? I find that a lady investigator has us under surveillance."

He paused and brought his pockmarked face close to Toni's. "Now, do you understand that I will go to any length necessary to find out what we're up against?"

The tip of the swagger stick slammed viciously into her solar plexus, leaving her gagging and gasping for air. Cain waited patiently the seven minutes it took for Toni to recover control of her breathing and pay attention to his questions.

"Why were you watching this building?"

"Screw off," she spat.

The swagger stick dug into her solar plexus with such force that she lost consciousness. Cain swore. He had not intended to lose time having to wait until she recovered. The woman was so damn maddening. But, he knew he would eventually get the information he wanted. The Nazis who taught him the techniques were experts with years of practice.

He left her alone for a while. When he returned, he could tell right away that she was faking. He wandered in as if he did not know better and started to tap her head very lightly with his swagger stick. She held out amazingly well, pretending not to feel the light taps, but Cain knew better. By now it would feel like she was being hit with a battering ram. Her head would feel as if it were being battered inside a bass drum. He could see the neck muscles tighten with each tap. Finally she began to scream.

"Now," he said with satisfaction. "Now, you will tell me what I want to know."

She was weeping uncontrollably. She nodded her head.

"Who will be coming?"

"Able Team."

"When?"

"They . . . they would be here by now."

That shook Cain. He would have thought he had more time. Surely it took longer than that to get to Minneapolis from Kansas City. Something was wrong.

"How many strong is Able Team?"

"Three."

He swung the stick onto the same spot on her head. She screamed.

"How many?"

"Only three. They should be studying this place right now."

It suddenly made sense. First send a spy. Then send three scouts. After that, bring in the main body of killers to wipe the place out. Of course, the scouts could easily arrive long before the main body. They did not have to wait until one fight was finished before moving on. Cain turned and sprinted from the soundproof interrogation room. He ran up to the communications room and strode in there.

"Get me our patrol leaders," Cain told the radioman.

The radio operator handed the unit commander a microphone.

"You're on both walkie-talkie channels," he told his commander.

"This is Cain."

He waited for two voices to acknowledge before continuing. "There should be three men out there scouting us. Locate them, but leave them alone. Don't move in until the main force moves in to attack. Take the scouts only if they spot you. Have you got that?"

Two voices acknowledged.

Cain left the radio room and decided to do a tour of interior defenses before returning to the interrogation room. When whoever it was attacked, they were going to get hit back much harder than they had ever been hit before. Cain was grinning like a death's head as he made his rounds of the old warehouse that had become the HIT headquarters.

"THAT'S THE BUILDING, according to the intel from the Bear," Lyons said.

It was a warehouse—old, brick and ugly. All three stories were living and training quarters for a Harassment Initiation Team. WAR had separate, more respectable offices farther uptown.

Pol grabbed the walkie-talkie out of Gadgets's hand.

"Let me try that," Pol demanded. "Little sister? Come in little sister."

There was no more response than for the fifty or more times that Gadgets had tried it. Pol handed it back.

"We're being watched," Lyons told his two team members. "Fade."

"I want to talk to someone from that joint," Pol said. His voice held an edge of steel that was usually completely hidden.

"We fade. Carefully." Lyons ordered.

"I'm going to grab one of those killers," Pol insisted. "Toni left word with the office that she has the place under surveillance and has her walkie-talkie with her. They've got her."

Lyons clamped a grip of steel on Politician's upper arm.

"We leave," he said sternly.

They strolled in silence until well clear of the area.

"I don't know why we were allowed to walk out of that ambush," Lyons said. "But we don't have much time. Let's pick up the heavy-duty artillery and make a sweep. We'll start with the soldiers covering the ambushers, then take the ambushers and then move in on the building. That's playing it by the book, but it stinks."

"Why *were* we allowed to walk?" Gadgets insisted.

"Maybe Toni didn't tell them anything," Pol said. His voice was a whisper.

"You know better than that," Lyons said.

"The drugs they have these days...." Gadgets added, trying to soften the cruel reality of Lyons's words.

The terror fighters were back at the van that Toni had left at the airport for them. It belonged to Able Group, the company owned by Schwarz and Blancanales, and managed by Toni Blancanales. The company specialized in industrial security. The van was one of its quick-response vehicles.

"I still smell something wrong," Lyons said as he fastened a web belt around his waist.

As soon as J. Courtney Cain left the interrogation room, Toni began working on the knots that held her. The goons who had tied her up were much more interested in letting their hands wander than in checking what they were doing. Toni had been able to tense her muscles and twist her arms. Now she relaxed and worked with the slack. It took time, time that she did not know whether she had. She had run into trouble before. Twice the big man, Mack Bolan, had come to her aid. She had learned from him and learned well. So she fought one battle at a time with total concentration, not allowing the uncertainty of the next minutes to rob her of her effectiveness.

Soon the knots gave and she was free. The next problem was to arm herself.

She opened the door a crack. No one was in the hall outside. She went back and picked up the wooden chair to which she had been tied. She smashed it against the cement floor again and again. Finally, she had a piece of the back of the chair that made a fairly passable club.

She was reasonably certain that her purse was still on the main floor, in Cain's office. Her objective was the purse for inside was a weapon and the walkie-talkie.

She met a terrorist-in-training running along the hall, M-16 in one hand and a sandwich in the other. She stepped in front of him and brought the club up into the goon's groin. As he bent forward, Toni grabbed a fistful of his grimy hair and yanked. The would-be terrorist crashed into the wall headfirst. Two hard blows with the club kept him on the floor.

Toni grabbed the M-16 and patted her victim down for spare clips. He carried only one. She jammed that in her belt and took off, checking the load and cocking the assault rifle as she ran.

The rest was easy. There was no one in the office. The walkie-talkie was still in her purse. So was the Heckler & Koch VP-70 that Pol insisted she carry. She sat down in the desk chair facing the door. She placed the automatic in her waistband, and the magazine for the M-16 on the desk. Then the M-16 was set down carefully, still cocked and ready to roar, pointing at the door, ready to be grabbed in an instant. Only then did she get out the walkie-talkie and start to call for Able Team.

THE BACKUP MEN who were meant to cover the retreat of those in the ambush went first. Able Team knew what they were looking for and they found them. The barely concealed automatic handguns left no mistake about the terrorists' identities. Politician removed one man with a garrote, so quickly and so savagely that the thin wire went right through the neck. The goon's dying kick booted his own head into the gutter.

Gadgets used his Gerber to efficiently sever the top of a spine. The killer collapsed without a sound. Lyons silently removed two more with his lethal fists.

The ambushers waited patiently, strung out along the tops of two buildings. They were still waiting when silenced .45 and 9mm slugs smashed heads. Able Team left them slumped over their guns and started back down a flimsy fire escape. Suddenly, Gadgets's walkie-talkie let out its discreet buzz.

Gadgets stopped so abruptly that Pol ran into him. Lyons noticed he was no longer being tagged by the rest of his team and carefully retreated. His eyes skimmed the territory for more enemy.

"Don't stop on the exposed escape," he hissed.

"That you, Toni?" Gadgets said.

"You were expecting someone else?" she replied.

The relief was too much to contain. Both Gadgets and Pol started to laugh.

"Where are you?" Toni's voice asked.

"Just ready to move in on the building. We had to take out an ambush first. Where are you?"

"Right here waiting, but you better try cutting out. Most of the force is in cars waiting for you to show signs of being in the area. The only thing that's stopping them from scooping you is that they're expecting a larger force."

"I wonder what gave them that notion?" Gadgets said.

"I wonder. I figured since I was foolish enough to get caught, it might as well serve some purpose."

Gadgets looked at Lyons who nodded.

"Sit tight. Here we come," he told Toni.

"Don't. It's a well-planned trap."

"You say they're all mobile?"

"Right."

"Great. Here we come. Out."

With the ambush out of the way, Lyons led his team right in the front door of the HIT headquarters. As they walked in, the first of the troop trucks could be seen turning a corner at the end of the block. Without warning from the ambushers, the reserves did not get tipped off until someone from the building saw Able Team walking up to the front door.

Lyons had the assault shotgun rigged with a 30-round drum. Pol carried his usual M-79 and a large supply of frag grenades for the launcher. Gadgets kept his Ingram at the ready.

Pol stayed at the door while Lyons and Gadgets investigated the reception area. Pol watched as two light trucks and a carload of troops stopped in front of the building. As soon as he saw weapons, he opened fire.

The fragmentation and white phosphorous grenades were carefully spread at his feet. He fired as quickly as he could reload. The first frag landed in the back of the truck, stunning those few it did not kill. The second went through the window of the car, taking out the unit commander and radioman. The next two grenades were phosphorous. They sprayed the men in the second car with fire that burned as it penetrated their bodies. In less than five seconds the street was a fiery hell, filled with the screams of the dying.

The only terrorists left inside the building were raw recruits. They were grouped around the communications room on the top floor.

When Able Team found Toni she smiled, picked up the M-16 and joined them. Gadgets found another contingent of mobile troops were covering the other entrance to the building.

He radioed Lyons who moved to the back of the second floor. Half of a 30-round drum of heavy pellets fired from the second-floor window reduced the backup terrorists to a mixture of gore and auto parts.

J. COURTNEY CAIN was a man who loved to talk. At this moment he would have preferred that others talk to him. First, he had lost contact with the sniping party. So, he had called the mobile troops and told them to move in cautiously. Both troops had reported moving right into the building. Then he had lost radio contact with both halves of his mobile pincers.

"Get me the interior patrol," he told the radio operator.

But firing burst out outside the door. He knew that the interior patrol would not answer either. He leveled his Colt Commander at the door and waited.

"Let head office know what's happening," he ordered the radioman.

Before the radio operator could respond, the knob of the door began to turn. Cain put a half clip through the door from bottom to top.

Politician saw the bullets stitch the terrorist who had tried to retreat into the room he was supposed to be guarding. Two shots from Lyons's assault shotgun cleared away the last of the guards on the top floor.

Politician and Toni approached the room together. Pol picked up an assault rifle and threw it against the door. Another hail of angry bullets flew out through the wood. Pol then booted the door. It split up the middle to reveal a small man in perfectly pressed fatigues, desperately trying to change clips with shaking hands. Behind him a radio operator frantically tried to raise someone to come to his aid.

Toni walked to the shattered door. "Goodbye, Commander," she said.

She emptied the clip into the small communications room. She spared one shot for the radio man. The rest of the bullets were used to perforate the carefully pressed fatigues.

16

"I said close the damn thing down. Destroy it!" Jishin screamed into the telephone.

The voice on the other end squawked in protest.

"Did you or did you not send the orders for simultaneous attacks yesterday?" Jishin demanded.

"I do believe you. That's why I'm telling you to wipe out that idiot computer. Someone's gotten to it."

She cut off the protests in midsentence. "It may be impossible, but it's been done. I've arranged by telephone for your office, Salt Lake City, Houston and Seattle to hold simultaneous attacks later today. I spoke to each group leader myself. I also told them to ignore any orders that came via the computer link. So close it down. I'll be there after the raids to see what went wrong."

She slammed down the telephone and turned to the Japanese terrorist standing next to her. "The idiots think they must see something happen with their own eyes before it really happened. I think the long nose puts undue strain on the brain."

The terrorist, who called himself Colonel Noh, laughed politely. "What is the target of our Boston team? We have ten professionals and lost only half the long-noses. We may as well expend the rest."

"We may as well, indeed," Jishin agreed. "Our target will not be synchronized. We're going to fly to Atlanta. So our strike will be later."

"Surely we have sufficient targets in the Boston area?"

"We have unfinished business in Atlanta," she snapped. "No one there will be expecting another raid. Elwood

Electronic Industries and that mongrel bitch that works for them will both go.''

July 14, 812 hours, Smyrna, Georgia

DEBORAH WANDERED into Ti's lab to find her throwing punches and kicks at the window glass.

"What on earth are you doing?" Deborah asked.

Ti looked around and grinned, like a kid caught playing in a puddle. "Making sure this tempered glass is as strong as it's supposed to be."

"I thought when they fixed the place up, Mr. Brognola had bullet-proof glass put in?"

"I believe it will stop light automatic fire, but will it stop human beings?" Ti questioned.

She dragged a heavy table over to a position four feet from the window.

"Did you see the sign on the door?" she asked Deborah.

"Yeah. That's why I came in. You're out of your mind."

"You're just in time. Brace the table."

"What?"

"The table. Keep it from moving away from the window."

Deborah dutifully put her shoulder to the table, spread her feet and pushed against it. Ti stood with her back to the window and her hands on the edge of the table. Suddenly she kicked her feet up into the air and then straight back in a mule kick that hit the center of the windowpane with a resounding bang. The window did not break, but Deborah and the heavy table moved back eight inches. Ti landed lightly on her feet.

"I'm sold. It's good glass."

"God," Deborah said, "to resist a kick like that, it's good steel."

Ti dusted her hands off. "Thank you. Now, you saw the sign on the door. I have to get ready for the meeting."

"Yeah. Well, I'm going to attend the meeting too," Devine said.

"But, it's scientific personnel only. You saw the sign on the door."

"Save it for someone who isn't in the business. You're the only scientific personnel left in this joint. That sign is nothing but an engraved invitation to the terrorists. I'll hang around, thank you."

Ti looked at the platinum blonde with a mixture of respect and affection.

"Sure?" Ti asked.

"Positive."

"Then let's start getting ready."

"What makes you so sure that they'll attack again today?"

"They turned their computer off at 5:06 this morning. But not before a telephone call from Jishin. I feel sure she'll be coming back here."

"Why?"

"It's a matter of face. She lost a great deal of face here. In her mind, she won't be able to regain her respect until she's returned here and destroyed whatever caused the loss of face."

"You?"

"Mostly, me," Ti admitted.

"Where do we begin?"

"Gadgets left some plastic explosive behind. I want booby traps. I also want to keep this place looking as if it were in full use."

"Let's do it," Deborah said.

July 14, 923 hours, Santa Clara, California

"WHAT WAS THAT?" Babette asked.

Hal Brognola pulled the cigar from his mouth and whispered. "Someone picking the lock on the door."

Babette quietly moved to the small desk and chair she had put into the office. She sat in the chair facing the door and pulled open the top drawer. She removed an Ingram Model 10, chambered a .45 round and put the weapon back, barrel forward in the open drawer.

Brognola moved against the wall to stand behind the door when it opened. He carefully placed the wooden chair in which he had been sitting so it would prevent the door from being slammed into him. He took out his VP 70Z and waited.

The lock on the door finally clicked back. The picker opened the door and stepped back.

"It's open, Fred."

"Then let's see what's in there."

The one called Fred took three paces into the room and stopped cold. His partner who picked locks almost bumped into him.

"Good morning, gentlemen," Babette said calmly. "Couldn't you have waited? The office opens at 9:30."

The two men had stopped exactly between Babette and Brognola. The one known as Fred brought his hand from his pants pocket. The hand was wrapped around a Colt 1911A1 automatic. He pointed it at Babette.

"Just freeze," he told her. "If that hand starts coming out of the drawer, I'll blow your head off."

Brognola tried to ease the door open. He was anxious to cross the doorway and get Babette out of the position where she was lined up with the two terrorists.

"Just what did you gentlemen want that meant you couldn't wait for the office to open?" Babette stalled.

"We want to see if you have a computer that could be connected to ours in some way. We seem to be having trouble," Fred answered. Then he spoke to his partner. "Orrie, go around the desk and take whatever she has her hand on in that drawer."

When Orrie made his move, Brognola stepped rapidly to the side, forcing the door to slam. Orrie turned and leaped at him. Brognola fired a short burst. The 9mm parabellums entered through the chin and throat. They exited through the back of the head, spraying bits of brain on the ceiling.

The front of the cheap desk erupted as Babette squeezed the trigger on the Ingram. Forty-five caliber slugs flew through the desk. A line of them stitched the gunman's groin, shoving him back across the room. He collapsed eight feet from where he had been standing. Babette removed the Model 10 from the drawer and finished the job with a single head shot.

The sound of shots erupted from somewhere else in the building.

"What's happening?" Babette asked.

Brognola was already checking the hall outside. There was no activity yet.

"When Ti telephoned to tell us that the main computer had been shut down, I guessed this might happen," Brognola admitted. "It's a very small step from concluding that your computer has been tampered with to deciding that the tamperers must be somewhere close by. I was hoping they wouldn't, but that was too much to hope for."

"I've figured the rest out," Babette said. "They've sent a small army to check out the building."

"You got it. Gadgets says you're deadly with that thing." He nodded at the Ingram.

"That's right," Babette said with a proud smile.

"If you're game, I'd like to do more than escape. This group of terrorists is probably planning to attack an industrial site when they finish with us. If we have to shoot our way out anyway, I'd prefer not to leave enough of them to do any further damage."

Babette shrugged. "Why not?"

Brognola clamped his cigar in his teeth and stuffed the jacket pockets of his impeccable gray suit with clips for both the Ingram and the Heckler & Koch automatic.

"There's a bandolier in the case," he told Babette. "I thought you might be short of pockets."

"Then you were expecting this?" she asked.

"I thought it was a possibility. I suggest we go straight for their training center and work our way out."

He picked up the telephone and put it back.

"They're serious. The lines are dead."

"The rope we used for returning the bodies is still in the corner. Why don't we go down that way?"

"That's what I call a surprise visit."

Brognola swung the gymnast on the end of the rope. She gained the ledge and quickly refastened the rope to the pitons she had driven into the building before. Brognola tied off the rope at the top and then slid down to join Babette outside the window to the computer room. A quick kick removed the glass.

Babette did a forward roll into the room and came up with the Ingram cocked and ready. Brognola followed. There was no sign of the regular workers. Instead, two men and a woman stood using citizen-band radios. Each had an M-16 slung over a shoulder. The breaking glass caused them to turn, but they were too taken by surprise to do more than look.

"Put those radios down slowly," Brognola told them.

The woman threw her radio at the big Fed and let the assault rifle slide from her shoulder into her hand. She was much too slow. Babette's chatter gun spat a figure eight of 250-grain sizzlers that drove the three back over desks.

Babette was already running toward the door to the hall. She threw it open and leaned around the doorway. A group of about a dozen terrorists were pounding up the hall toward the sound of the firing. They already had their guns out.

Babette emptied the rest of her clip into the running horde, then jerked back inside just as bullets from the opposite direction chewed up the doorway.

Brognola stood and listened to the group charge from the other end of the hall. Babette moved clear of the fire zone as she quickly changed clips.

When he heard the footsteps slow down at the door, Brognola emptied his clip through the wall. He was rewarded with a chorus of screams.

"The training center is one floor down," Babette yelled as she moved out the door.

Three short bursts finished the terrorists.

The third floor was in better order. The terrorists, organized by their instructors, were just setting off to help search the building. It had taken a while to convince them that destroying all they found was basically sound policy, but now they were psyched up and ready. Their first two identifiable enemies stepped through the door from the stairs and stood back to back in the busy hall.

It was a sight to make anyone pause: a senior executive, complete with cigar and three-piece gray suit, standing spread legged and firm, glowering over a vicious-looking machine pistol; standing straight behind him, a blonde wearing slacks, shirt and bandolier, looking equally efficient with her gun.

"Who are you?" someone asked.

"Justice," Brognola growled.

The two Ingrams then explained his remark. Bodies were swept toward the far ends of the hall. The one or two terrorists who did manage to shoot succeeded only in cutting up the terrorists who were packed against them. There were four seconds of thunder and destruction. Then the sound of empty clips hitting the floor and new clips being slammed home could be heard in the hall.

Brognola then led the way to a door marked: Harassment Initiation Team—Members Only.

He threw open the door and found terrorists, each wearing a white *gi* and white belt. They were obviously scared, raw recruits, all unarmed.

"Let's let them go," he said. He and Babette headed down the stairs.

They threw their Ingrams into the back seat of the car that Brognola had left waiting. Then they climbed in and sped away from the sound of approaching sirens.

"Want to come to Atlanta and share the reports on the rest of the operation?" the Fed asked.

"Damn right," snapped the reply.

17

Yakov Katzenelenbogen let the telephone ring twice before cutting into the line. It was about time, he thought—he had been wrapped around the telephone junction box for two hours. He had been starting to think that the terrorists were too depraved to notice that their toilets did not work.

"Yes," Katz answered into the lineman's mouthpiece.

"Comfort Plumbing?" a gruff man's voice asked.

"Yes, sir. What can I do for you."

"All our damn drains are backing up. We got no toilets working. How soon can you do something about it?"

"Where are you, sir?"

The goon gave him the address. "Okay," Katz said, "I was just leaving to do an installation almost next door. I'll be there real soon."

"That's terrific."

Katz hung up.

He quickly unhooked his telephone-line patch and threw it into the large, canvas tool bag he had. He tossed the bag into a rented van and sat down to wait. He was in sight of the building where the Seattle Harassment Initiation Team was getting its briefing. He had visited the building during the night. He had flitted throughout the terrorist lair, learning the layout and flushing crepe-de-chine bags of flax seed down all the toilets. The expanding flax would have clogged every drain in the place by now. Katz chuckled as he started the van.

Bert Bannon waited impatiently at the door of the old industrial building. The briefing on today's raid had already begun and he had wanted to hear it. Instead, he had to keep an eye on the plumber. He sighed.

He was watching as a van stopped right at the door. An old man got out. Then Bert noticed the steel hook where the right hand should be. The guy swung a canvas bag of tools onto his shoulder. The bag looked like a relic from the Civil War. The bag was packed, yet he seemed to handle it easily enough.

"You from Comfort?" Bert asked as the old man came in the door.

"Yes. Where are the drains that are giving you trouble?"

"Every damn toilet in the place is plugged. We're going ape."

"Then let's start at the top floor and work down."

"Ahh. . . . There's a meeting going on up there. Why not start on the second floor?"

"And if we free the toilets on the second floor and then get a back-up when we unclog the top floor, who cleans up the mess?" the old man asked.

Bert did not like it. If the old geezer overheard too much, Bert would have to kill him. Still, that would be easier than cleaning up the second floor.

"Come on. I'll stay with you," Bert told the plumber.

Most of the top floor was open area. In one corner were the washrooms and in another was an office area. The partitions were old, sturdily built with two-by-four studs and board walls, carefully finished and stained dark. The many hanging fluorescent fixtures did little to dispel the gloom of the place.

A flip chart had been set up near one wall and about forty men sat on stacking chairs listening to a briefing.

"Commander Jishin has been on the telephone to me again this morning," the man at the front was saying. "We all begin our strikes at eleven hundred hours, local time. So be sure you have this straight. We won't be going over it again."

Bert impatiently tugged the old man toward the washrooms. "Come on, this way."

The plumber went into the men's bathroom. Bert followed. He looked away in disgust. Several of the men had used the toilets and tried to flush them. The floor was wet.

"That's your trouble," the plumber said. His voice was suddenly authoritative.

"Huh?"

"Too much shit around here," the old man said.

Suddenly the hook was a blur. The hard metal cracked into the temple. Bert Bannon slumped forward, his knees buckled and he collapsed. His last breaths were taken with his head immersed in an overflowing toilet.

Katz calmly went about his business. First he removed the sections of a tripod from his tool bag. When he had assembled the tripod, he carried it outside the washroom and placed it in a clear area about ten feet from the door.

The commander delivering the briefing was telling his troops, "We want lots of blood and lots of misery. You don't make headlines by being neat and clean."

Katz returned to the can. In a moment he came out lugging a pair of motorcycle batteries and leads.

There were a few whispers when some sort of Gatling gun was carried out and set on the tripod. An ammo belt was dragged after it, the first bullet already locked in the breech. Katz quickly connected the leads from the batteries to the electric motor on the gun that was designed primarily for helicopter use. The belt held standard 7.62 by 51mm NATO ammunition. The gun was capable of chewing up ten of those rounds each second and spitting them through one of the six rotating barrels at 2850 feet per second.

By the time the Phoenix Force leader grabbed the twin handles and began to swing the machine gun, the terrorists were beginning to suspect that all was not well. Mutters rose, attracting the attention of the speaker. He had time to glance in the direction of the distraction before the GE Minigun began delivering death. An entire row of heads received 150-grain goodbyes.

Some of the terrorists dived onto the floor while they fumbled for handguns. They were swept up with bullets. Others tried to outrun death, but failed. A few made it to the office. They could have saved the effort. The machine-gun fire did not seem to realize there was anything there. It swept through the two-by-four and wood partitions, leveling terrorists.

A minute and a half later, when the last round had quieted the last groan, Katz was the only one moving. He carried the canvas tool bag to the Minigun and quickly disassembled it and put it back in the bag. Then, easily throwing the eighty-five pounds of gear on his shoulder, he produced an Uzi and headed for the stairs.

No one tried to stop him.

Katz threw his bag of tools into the rented van and drove away. No one was remotely curious about an old trades-man leaving an old building.

July 14, 1012 hours, Houston, Texas

THE COMMANDER of the Texas Harassment Initiation Team looked over his men. He was proud of them. He had recruited and trained them himself. He was about to prove that he was worth every cent of the three thousand dollars a week he had been paid. This unit was not about to fall on its face like some of the others had. He decided to make his summary of the briefing extremely short.

"Remember, *A* and *B* teams close in on the target. First, eliminate all the workers except the computer scientists—we'll use drugs to debrief them later. Then let the specialists take what they need from both the electronic and paper files before you destroy and retreat.

"*C* and *D* teams, you have the more difficult job. Someone is going to try to stop us. You are to keep a quarter-mile circumference around *A* and *B* teams at all times, during the raid and during the travel to and from. The moment another force tries to hit *A* and *B* teams, you close in and eliminate. Is everything clear?"

No one said anything.

"Then get to your assigned cars and let's put the show on the road."

Houston is a city where no one moves without a car.

HIT had their office and training center outside the 610 circle, near Genoa Airport. They had their own cinder-block building and parking lot. In the lot the group leaders began directing the men to their assigned transportation.

The last man was out of the building and the first car was moving out of the gate of the parking compound when the machine gun on the roof opened fire.

Tracers zeroed in on the engine of the lead car, bringing it to a standstill in the middle of the exit gate. The tracers then probed the back of the car until they found the gas tank. The only two terrorists to escape the inferno were cut down within inches of the car.

From a rooftop over five hundred yards away another light machine gun opened fire. A three-round burst perforated every terrorist who tried to regain the door to the building. Soon the door was well blockaded by the bodies piled against it.

"Take out those gun emplacements!" The command was shouted from between two cars. It was easier to issue the command than it was to perform the feat. Every time a head showed, a three-round burst went through the vehicle and the body behind it.

The tracers continued to stream from the roof of the terrorist stronghold. Gas tank after gas tank ruptured into a geyser of flames. Soon commands could no longer be heard over the screams of the dying. Two minutes later, the only sound in the enclosed parking lot was the crackle of flames and the pings of stretching metal.

Gary Manning on the roof of the terrorist hideout gave the thumbs-up sign to David McCarter who had been doing the sharpshooting from the roof of the more distant building. McCarter grinned and waved.

Both quickly picked up their Heckler & Koch HK21E machine guns and began their retreat. McCarter used his paratroop training to jump from the low building, cradling the machine gun in his arms. He held it almost tenderly, thinking that he could have done the same high-accuracy job from twice the distance with that beautifully machined, twenty-two inch barrel. He laid the gun on the back seat of a rented Lincoln and peeled rubber to the front of the HIT building.

Manning came around the corner and put his Heckler & Koch HK21E on top of McCarter's. He then threw a couple of jackets over the hardware and climbed into the front. The first siren could be heard faintly.

"Piece of cake," Manning said as he moved sedately away from the building.

"Let's go get us some Houston hospitality." McCarter grinned.

18

July 14, 1050 hrs, Salt Lake City, Utah

A weary Carl Lyons sat at the back of the Stony Man executive jet.

Rosario Blancanales walked back toward him.

"Carl, Katz's on the blower," he said. "He's got bad news."

Lyons grumbled to himself all the way up the aisle of the plane. He collapsed into the copilot seat without acknowledging Jack Grimaldi. He snatched up the microphone and growled into it.

"Yeah, Katz."

"I just came from a get-together in Seattle," Katz said, his voice sounding scratchy through the descrambler. "Old Ma Jishin's been gossiping on the telephone again. Time for all raids is now eleven hundred hours, local time."

Lyons glanced at his watch. "That's six minutes from now."

"Right."

Lyons glanced at Grimaldi, whose fingers were flying over his custom flight computer. He did not have to ask the question.

Grimaldi reported. "I can have you over Anderson Androids, the most probable target, in eleven minutes. Can we get a confirm?"

"You going to stand this can on its tail again?"

"Why not? It's fun."

Lyons spoke into the mike again. "Katz, we can reach the target about five minutes after hit time. We need a monitor on the police channels and a confirmation of the target."

"I'll arrange for the police to give it to you. That way

they'll be expecting some 'experts.' You have ID if they ask?''

"I'll dig it out. Thanks, Katz."

"No problem. Out."

Lyons went back to Pol and Gadgets.

"Let's get ready. We'll have to walk the rest of the way. Soft armament. The wolves are going to reach the sheep first. Try the gray jump suits and use body armor."

All members of Able Team scrambled to equip themselves and be ready in time to jump.

"Why gray?" Gadgets asked as he put on the jump suit over the custom-made flak suit with its heating-cooling system.

Lyons was selecting ID folders from an attaché case full. He passed two out to his teammates and pocketed one himself.

"Just a hunch. The most probable target is one of these modern ultrasecure places with no windows."

"Got you," Pol answered. "Good thinking."

"I'm packing extra Gerber Mark 1's," Gadgets remarked.

"We may need C-4. Pack lots," Lyons told Gadgets. "Also dig out those infrared flashlights and the goggles that go with them."

"Those damn things must weigh five pounds," Pol complained.

"I'm going to carry an Ingram," Gadgets said.

"No .45s! Uzis with disintegrating ammo and flash suppressors for everyone," Lyons barked. "Move it. We must be about there. Silenced Beretta 93-Rs in the shoulder rigs. Stun grenades only."

Grimaldi stuck his head around the door to the flight deck. "Probable target confirmed. I dump you in 150 seconds from. . . now. Good luck."

Able Team nodded. Their mental clocks were counting down as they scrambled into the parachutes.

OFFICER PAT MALONE and his partner, Officer Inez Gallic, were the first to answer the report of explosions and gunfire in a new industrial park, east of the University of

Utah. It was in one of the new buildings, Anderson Androids Ltd.

The terrorist techniques had been crude, but effective. They had gone to the only entry—it consisted of an outside door, a very small entrance hall, and two electronic doors that led farther into the building—opened the outer door and tossed in a large bundle of explosive. They had then ducked back out and braced the outer doors. The force of the explosion in the small foyer had blown both of the security doors right off their hinges, but the outside doors, which had been braced, were still functional.

Now the terrorists had automatic rifles covering the only entrance to the building. There were not even any windows that could be broken for entry. The building was nothing more than a very fancy concrete box. Those inside were completely dependent on artificial lighting, and air-conditioning.

Inez finished on the radio to headquarters and walked back to where Malone was covering the entrance to the building with his service revolver.

"SWAT on its way?" Malone asked.

His partner shook her head. "Federal specialists be here in another four minutes. Reinforcements are putting up a containment net, but we're to stay out of the building."

"Suits me."

The sky was suddenly filled with the scream of a black jet. The jet, much larger than a fighter, sizzled over the horizon from a low altitude and then began to climb straight up over the industrial park. The engines suddenly flamed out. The plane slowed until it hung motionless in the sky, only about fifteen hundred feet over the building.

"God!" the female cop exclaimed. "It's going to crash right about here."

Just when the plane was almost still, three black forms appeared by the tail. Then the plane lost its grip on the sky. It slipped to one side and came rushing at the earth, left wing first.

Officers Pat Malone and Inez Gallis threw themselves flat on the carefully manicured lawn of the building they were watching. Then they rolled on their side to watch the plane fall toward them.

Slowly, slowly, the left wing began to drag and the nose came forward. Then, with a puff of smoke, the two engines burst into ignition. The plane continued its earthward course, pushed by two huge turbojets attached to the body just behind the wings.

Suddenly the nose began to lift. The plane bottomed out of its dive and screamed away less than fifty feet from the tops of the buildings.

"I didn't see that," Malone said. His voice shook.

Then he remembered the three black forms. He looked back at the spot where the plane had hung motionless in the sky and was surprised to see that three parachutes were already beginning to billow open.

"That isn't really possible, is it?" Inez asked.

"I'm sure it's not," Malone confirmed.

The three jumpers landed perfectly on the soft sod of the company lawn. A tall blond man unsnapped his chute and ran toward the two police officers. They waited, still not quite believing what they were seeing.

The man stood well over six feet tall. He had a shock of blond hair peeking out from under a gray watch cap. His fatigues were gray and there was gray skin cover smeared carelessly on his face. A deadly looking Uzi with a flash suppressor rode on his right thigh in a quick-release clip.

"Malone and Gallic?" The voice was clipped, the words impatient.

"Yes," Malone answered.

"You were told to expect us."

Malone grinned. "Didn't expect anything quite so dramatic. Where's the rest of the crew?"

Carl Lyons gestured to the other two jumpers. Like their leader, they had unsnapped their chutes and let the wind have them. They were consulting a piece of paper and finding a particular spot on the cement wall at one side of the building.

"Just the three of you?"

Cold eyes ignored the question.

"You may need backup," Lyons said. "You might find terrorists coming out this door. I would advise placing yourself against the wall and shooting anyone who comes out the door with a weapon in his or her hand."

"You're kidding."

"I don't kid," Lyons replied.

He then turned his back on the two cops and began to walk around the building. At the next corner Lyons found the power lines leading into the building. He emptied a clip from the Uzi into the connectors. The power lines fell free, crackling their charge into the grass.

"Can either of you throw a grenade?" Lyons asked the cops when he came back.

Gallic nodded. "I was pretty good in the army."

Lyons pulled two concussion grenades off his webbing.

"Get your partner to hold the door. Toss both these in and get the door shut when I give you the sign."

He left them standing waiting at the only door to the building. Gallic stood where she could see up the side of the building. Malone stood where he could grab the door.

"Now!" yelled his partner.

He yanked the door open and two grenades sizzled past him into the small entrance area. He let go of the door and ran along the front of the building. Automatic fire from inside was so late that it succeeded only in bouncing from the heavy glass of the closing door.

Then the two grenades blasted the door back open. From the side of the building came the sharp crack of another explosion. Malone held his position, revolver trained on the exit. He was relieved to see a riot truck screaming up to the building.

"What's happening?" he yelled to Inez.

"They blasted a hole in the side of the building. I never saw people move so fast. They were all inside before the rubble stopped falling."

Malone shook his head. Only three of them. They were going to have to move faster than bullets. How the hell were they going to get the hostages out in the dark?

The inside of the building was not dark. As soon as the

power was cut, the emergency generator had cut in. Between batteries and the latest technology, the power pickup had been so smooth that it was not even noticeable.

Able Team came into a large storeroom as Gadgets had planned. Even here, one emergency light bulb burned.

"Kill it," Lyons ordered.

Gadgets unscrewed the light bulb and spit on the base. He then balanced a quarter over the bulb and screwed it back into the socket.

"That should kill the local fuse," he reported.

The three warriors put on the infrared goggles. When Pol turned on his infrared flashlight, it showed the door quite plainly.

They moved cautiously out of the storage room.

"More light to the left," Lyons said. "Gadgets, find that emergency generator and take it out."

"It doesn't show on the sketchy building plan that we were sent. I'll stick with you until we find the elevators. The stairs to the basement are close to the elevator well."

The three warriors started to jog down a corridor toward the center of the building.

Suddenly two terrorists appeared around a corner. They were dragging a struggling woman between them. Politician was closest to the two goons. The stick in his hand whistled and bounced off the temple of one. He dropped.

The second terrorist spun, bringing his M-16 up as he turned. He was far too slow. The stick bounced back over the head of the victim and poked the terrorist in the throat. He fell back unable to even call out. Politician followed through by grabbing the other end of the *jo* in his left hand and pressing the stick across the terrorist's windpipe. In a moment he was backed up against the corridor wall, fighting to take the crushing pressure from his air supply.

"Where is the main force?" Politician asked.

"Go to hell," he choked.

"I can tell you that," the woman said.

As soon as she spoke, Lyons's Beretta let out a quiet gasp. The terrorist under Pol's stick acquired a hole in his temple. He folded like a deck chair.

"When these creeps hit, everyone headed for the top floor and barricaded the doors. These killers are still trying to get through the barricade. I hid on this floor. I was trying to sneak out to telephone the police, but they were watching the emergency door as well as the main one."

"I thought there was only one door," Gadgets said.

She shook her head. "There's one that looks like a cement block. It only opens from the inside."

"Pol, let's start picking off enemy," Lyons said. "Gadgets, get those lights."

Gadgets turned to the woman. "Can you find the emergency generator?"

She nodded.

"Let's go."

Gadgets and the woman went down a flight of metal stairs. Lyons and Politician turned around to go up. Suddenly an explosion washed down the steps, nearly knocking them off their feet.

"The terrorists are on the third floor now," Lyons said grimly. He started to take the stairs quickly, in spite of the noise he made.

Gadgets and the woman reached a subbasement. She threw her light weight into opening the heavy door at the foot of the stairs and almost got herself killed. A hail of bullets deflected from the partly open door and whined around the concrete stairwell.

Gadgets leaped down the last four stairs and slammed his weight against the door to close it. Then he quickly pulled the pin from a concussion grenade and opened the door just enough to toss it in.

The muffled whump of the grenade started opening the heavy door. Gadgets helped it open farther. He already had the Uzi out of its clip and ready. Two terrorists did a brief death shuffle as a figure-eight burst finished the job the stun grenade had begun.

"You sure move fast," the woman breathed.

Gadgets grinned as he quickly disabled the emergency generator.

"As soon as the power was cut off, they must have sent

these two to protect the generator. They're very efficient," the woman mused.

Gadgets adjusted the infrared goggles. They were uncomfortable, but necessary. Then with the Uzi in one hand and the infrared projector in the other, he instructed the woman. "Grab my belt. I'll lead you to a way out. If I start shooting or someone starts shooting at us, hit the floor. I'll come back for you."

"Ahh, okay." Some of her confidence seemed to have gone with the light.

He pushed on the heavy door. A bright light hit the infrared goggles, almost blinding him because of the built-in amplification. He rolled away from the door as bullets dug at the doorframe.

"This the only entrance to the generator room?" Gadgets asked the woman.

"Yeah," she confirmed in a shaky voice.

Lyons and Politician were half a flight from the blasted door when the emergency light went out. Two terror goons had been left behind to prevent victims from escaping the top floor. Lyons continued up the stairs.

He surprised the pair with two small flashes and low coughs from a silenced gun at point-blank range. For those two killers the darkness became permanent.

Pol caught up to Lyons and the pair moved quietly through the carpeted halls of the high-tech building. Their infrared goggles separated humans from background. In the infrared light they could tell whether the person was armed. Armed terrorists met a karate blow to the temple or a single 9mm parabellum.

Workers were told in whispers that the stairs were clear for now. They were told to crawl to the stairwell and get out of the fire zone.

Ten minutes of silent confusion reigned on the top floor. The trickle of evacuees became a flow. The bodies of terrorists began to litter the halls.

Then, a match flared over a body. Politician's Uzi was leveled in an instant, but he held his fire. He could not tell what innocents might be farther down the hall. He broke into a run toward the terrorist, but the match went out and the goggles took two seconds to readjust to the lower intensity of infrared light. By the time Pol could see, the terrorist had leaped into a side room and was yelling.

"We've been infiltrated. Retreat. Everyone out."

Lyons and Pol were caught out of position. They had moved forward with speed and efficiency, eliminating terrorists and helping potential hostages to escape. When the shouting began, they were separated and far from the stairwell.

Politician still could not risk the Uzi because he could not see to the end of the hall behind the goons. Terrorists burst out of a room right beside him, and he lost his infrared light in the scramble. He still had the *jo* tucked into the back of his web belt. He slammed the Uzi back into its clip and drew the fighting stick.

He was among the goons, sweeping and jabbing. Four went down, but eight or nine made it into the stairwell. Then the scene became lighter and he knew that Lyons was back with his infrared light. The rest of the terrorists began to crumple as silent bullets kissed them goodbye, one at a time. Pol did not dare take a weapon out without his light to identify him. He raised his hands and *jo* into the air.

"I see you, Rosario. Lose your light?"

"Yeah. Eight or nine terrorists are on those stairs between us and the workers."

Lyons wasted no breath. He ran for the stairwell, leaving Pol to fend for himself.

GADGETS WENT INTO a crouch by the heavy door.

"Pull it open," he commanded his guide.

She yanked the door open, keeping herself behind it. Gadgets laid a pattern of 9mm tumblers around the light. It dropped to the floor. Another bullet turned it off. Then Gadgets's infrared goggles went back over his eyes and he charged into the stairwell. He perforated both blurs and then turned on the infrared light to check. Both were dead. He jammed a fresh clip into the Uzi as he returned to hook his guide to his belt.

When they reached the ground floor, Gadgets noiselessly detached himself from the woman and indicated for her to wait. He then went into the office area by the main door. Three terrorists spun to see who was approaching.

Squinting against the sudden light, Gadgets sprayed the area with the entire clip. Only one terrorist managed to pull the trigger on his M-16. He sprayed a neat figure eight into the ceiling as he fell backward with two manglers in his chest.

Gadgets returned to the woman. "Go to the door," he said. "Tell them not to shoot. Then go out and tell the police to expect more workers soon." She nodded and went.

Gadgets went back to the hall and let his eyes adjust to the faint light of the goggles before moving on. By that time the first escapees from the top floor began to appear. It took only a few seconds to start the chain going out of the building. Then Gadgets began slowly moving against the flow of refugees toward the top floor.

A voice suddenly rang out from half a floor up. "They're on the stairs below us. Spray the stairs."

Gadgets shoved the last two stragglers behind him. Then he pointed the Uzi upward and waited to locate the muzzle-flashes. But before the terror goons could open fire, two concussion grenades dropped from above, scattering them along the steps. Then Lyons closed in from the top and Gadgets from the bottom.

"I think that takes care of things," Gadgets called up the stairs before coming into line with Lyons's Uzi.

Gadgets was ambushed as he emerged from the building and stood blinking in the bright light. Arms and legs wrapped around him and a big kiss was planted on his mouth while long red hair whipped around his head.

"You're fabulous," the redhead he had led out of the building said in a throaty voice. "What can I ever do to repay you?"

"You got a car?"

"Yes."

"How about a ride to the airport for myself and my friends."

The redhead turned to a man in a gray suit who was standing a discreet five feet away.

"Have my car brought around, please."

"Right away, Miss Anderson."

"Did I hear, Miss Anderson?" Pol asked. "Are you related to the founder of this company?"

"*I*'m the founder," she replied with a grin.

Officer Gallic came up. "One of you called Ironman?"

Lyons nodded.

"Got a call patched through for you from California. You can get it in the cruiser."

It was Brognola.

"Wrapped things up here," the Fed said. "Houston and Seattle are taken care of. How did business go there?"

"A couple of casualties, but better than expected. Who got Jishin?"

"Didn't you?"

"No sign of her. Who's at Elwood Electronics?"

Brognola's voice sounded worried, even through the static. "Only Ti and Deborah."

"Out." Lyons shouted and jumped from the car.

He turned to Inez Gallic. "Run interference to the airport for us."

Able Team scrambled into the waiting Chrysler and took off after the police cruiser.

19

July 14, 1600 hours, Smyrna, Georgia

This time Jishin did not risk tipping anyone off to the raid by hijacking transportation from the airport. She hired two buses to move both the experienced foreign terrorists and the American terrorists-in-training from the airport to Elwood Electronic Industries Inc.

The buses pulled up to the plant. Two of the least certain of the trainees were left with the drivers. Their orders were to keep the drivers on the spot and out of the way. The other sixty-one terrorists divided into three groups to enter by the plant's three doors.

Jishin went with the group that used the front entrance. There was no one in the reception area. Two lights glowed on the switchboard, showing lines in use. The receptionist's typewriter was on and humming.

Beyond the reception area was the main office bull pen. The coffee was hot. Typewriters and copiers were on. A cigarette burned itself out in an ashtray.

"Creepy," said one of the recruits.

The others looked around and under desks, trying to ignore the remark.

"You three start on those files," Jishin ordered. "You four go back and cover the entry. You two see that the other teams have left their entries guarded as well. The rest of you find out where everyone's gone."

The terrorists scattered to obey orders.

Each of the three detailed to sort through files pulled open the top drawer of one of the upright cabinets. Each began scanning for anything pertaining to original research. The one in the middle found nothing but invoices in the top drawer. She slammed it shut and yanked open the second drawer. The three filing cabinets blew up, filling the room with sharp pieces of flying metal. Three terrorists died, four others experienced the pain of being severely wounded.

Jishin was not hit. She was already on her way to the computer room to see how things were going there. She heard the explosion and the screams but kept going. Someone would catch up with the details all too soon.

She found the terrorists wandering around the computer room. They looked lost.

"What's going on here?" Jishin demanded.

"Jobs are running. The computers are being worked but no one's here," someone reported in a puzzled voice.

"So what!" Jishin screamed. "Just get on with it."

They hastily moved in on the computer keyboards and started deciphering entry codes and working at a way to acquire the classified data.

Jishin stomped out in disgust, through the security and noise barriers, to the back of the building to discover what happened to the third part of the invading force. There was a sharp *crack* somewhere in a remote part of the building.

Jishin found the final third of her army frantically trying to dig their fellow workers out from under a heavy load of transformer cores and shelving.

"What do you think you're doing?" she barked.

The terrorists stopped and looked up.

"Tanna and Brian hit a trip wire and the shelves fell in on them."

Jishin stopped and picked up a discarded M-16. She jacked a shell into the chamber and fired two short bursts, killing the two imprisoned terrorists.

"That's what happens to careless types. Now, move it, before I lose patience. Find out what happened to the people who were working here."

Two messengers finally caught up with their leader.

"What do you two want?" she snapped at them.

"The file cabinets in the general office exploded," the

first reported. "We have three dead and four wounded."

"The tape drive in the computer room also blew up," the other reported. "We have two more seriously wounded."

Before Jishin could react, someone yelled. "Gas!"

Jishin recognized the harsh, burning sensation of strong ammonia in her nostrils.

"Clear the area," she barked.

In their haste to make it to the front of the building, the terrorists began to push and shove. That was when the lights went out.

There was still plenty of light streaming in the windows, but the power failure was the last straw for the already terrified killers. Their anger turned on each other. Soon fists were flying, the terrorists urgently wanting to quit the ammonia-filled stockrooms.

Jishin was still holding the M-16. She fired it into the air.

When she had sufficient attention, she spoke. "The next person I see shoving, gets shot."

The evacuation was immediately more orderly, but Jishin was forced to tie up her time standing in the ammonia-filled room, eyes streaming water, fighting not to cough, while her troops scrambled out the single door into the other parts of the building.

The terrorists in the general office area quickly patched up their wounded, leaving the dead where they lay. There was a brief argument about which eight would carry the wounded to a bus and which four would stay behind. It was settled that all would head for the buses, three carrying each wounded.

The buses were not there.

The two terrorists left to keep an eye on the bus drivers had remained behind. Each was carefully stretched out on the parking lot, his neck broken and his weapon missing.

It was too much for three of the terrorists-in-training. They dropped their wounded comrade and sprinted away from the menacing, silent building that seemed to be functioning, but in which no one could be found. They did not make it. One of the confiscated M-16s opened up, cutting them down with three short bursts.

None of the terrorists tried to return fire. They were tasting terror instead of dispensing it. They dropped their wounded and retreated back inside the building. The last one in slammed the door and then looked in horror at the string tied to the door handle. On the end of the string was a grenade pin. In the hush, all nine survivors heard the spoon fall with a clatter. Three were killed by the blast, two more were severely injured.

When Jishin found her first contingent of terrorists, the ones she had entered the building with, they were grouped in the reception area, ignoring the wounded at their feet. They were all crouched and waving weapons around, terrified, unable to find anything to shoot at.

After much bullying and commanding, Aya Jishin got the nine quaking terrorists to move and join the group in the computer room. They arrived at the double glass windows and looked into the soundproofed area just in time to see two grenades go off. The defensive grenades threw wire throughout the room, killing six and injuring several more, but the blast did not destroy the tempered glass of the viewing windows.

A close-up view of their companions being lacerated with thousands of pieces of wire was too much for the already cowering terrorists. They dropped their weapons and ran for the nearest door.

The group that had encountered the high concentrations of ammonia gas had cleared their eyes. It had taken much sponging and washing, but they were ready to continue their conquest of Elwood Electronics.

Then suddenly an M-16 started to chatter, spraying bullets into their ranks. The terrorists dived for whatever cover they could find and brought their own weapons up. They were all set when their fleeing companions charged through the room on their way to the door. All nine were cut down before the terrorists realized they were shooting their own people.

When the terrified goons began to stampede, Jishin went

after them. She saw the M-16 that provoked the firing. It had poked out above one of the sound-suppressing ceiling tiles.

"The enemy is above you!" Jishin yelled. "Watch the ceiling."

They responded immediately, chopping the tiles over their heads with .223 tumblers. Then they leaped on anything available, ready to establish a beachhead in the new war zone.

The sound of a low-flying jet boomed overhead. Jishin's battle instincts flared. A quick count told her that eighteen able-bodied troops were after the sniper or snipers in the crawl space. That was more than enough. Aya Jishin took off to find the other terrorists and move them outside to meet a new threat.

LAO TI AND DEBORAH DEVINE had had a busy afternoon. They had kept machines running, freshened coffee in cups, lit cigarettes and left them in ashtrays, coming back later to butt them and mess the ashes, and done many other small things to make the building look as if it was in use. Ti knew their survival required a psychological edge.

They also booby-trapped files and planned their own movements and routes to pick off the stragglers without exposing themselves to counterattack.

When the terrorists finally arrived, Deborah and Ti found themselves working like a well-trained team.

Ti waited in the crawl space for some of the traps to cause confusion. Deborah slipped outside, jogged over to the buses and easily took out the two amateur guards. After that, it took very little persuading to convince the bus drivers that they should leave.

Deborah then picked up the guards' M-16s and spare clips. Able Team had left weapons as well as grenades and explosives behind, but Deborah and Ti both preferred the psychological effect of using the enemy's own weapons against them.

Deborah delivered one weapon to Ti and then returned

to the parking lot and waited for the wounded to be delivered to the buses, which were no longer there.

Ti heard the file drawers blow up. She was already in position over the storerooms. When someone hit a trip wire and the shelves collapsed on top of the goons, she dropped the bottles of ammonia where they would do the most damage.

She then had managed to slip into the reception room and rig the grenade booby trap while the wounded were being carried to the parking lot.

Ti had also dropped the two grenades into the computer room, timing the blasts to occur just as the frightened terrorists arrived from the office area. She then had to scramble into position to start the shooting war between the two groups of terrorists. She had not counted on one side being so frightened that they dropped their weapons. Her psychological war was more effective than she had imagined.

When Ti heard Jishin shouting that the enemy was above, she knew she had lost more than her psychological edge.

DEBORAH DEVINE WAS outside the building. She witnessed the breathtaking stall of the black jet and the parachute exit of Able Team. Her rapt attention was broken by the sudden charge of terrorists out the loading doors of the building.

She quickly faded from sight. She had only one full clip of ammunition for the M-16 in her hands. The terrorists were already spreading around the perimeter of the parking lot, preparing a trap for the parachuting fighters.

Able Team was drifting on a beautifully controlled descent, headed straight for the largest open space in the parking lot.

Deborah could not wait while they dropped into the trap. She charged, determined to wipe out as large a circle of killers as she could. At the least, the gunfire would attract the attention of the jumpers.

Two terrorists were crouching in long grass. When Able Team was on the ground, the two killers would have a choice field of fire. Deborah emptied the clip from her M-16 into the pair. She stopped and snatched up the dead men's assault rifles.

Two more terrorists were crouched behind a parked car. Half a clip of tumblers taught them to dance before dying.

Deborah continued at a dead run, not daring to stop.

Three terrorists had their guns pointed at her. She dived into a ditch with tumblers crackling over her head. Jishin and three more killers were there, waiting.

Deborah reacted immediately. She swung her rifle butt into the face of the first terrorist, knocking him backward into one of his companions. Jishin was on her like a flash, plucking the rifle from her grip. Jishin then caught the wrist that was still outstretched and did a circular twist, levering the arm behind Deborah's back.

A sudden shove and Deborah Devine found herself staggering into the exposed area of the parking lot with no cover and no shelter.

Bullets riddled her body.

As SOON AS JISHIN had shouted, Lao Ti sprinted for another area of the crawl space. She flipped a ceiling tile out of place and found herself over an empty office. She carefully lowered herself and hung by one hand while she replaced the tile. The shooting had stopped. The goons would be cautiously poking into the attic at this point.

Ti had left the empty weapon behind. She moved quickly, knowing she had to either find a weapon or stay out of sight. She could hear the shouts of the terrorists, muffled sounds through the ceiling tiles.

Suddenly a ceiling tile was thrown aside in the hall she was traveling. A head poked down six feet ahead of her. "There's our target!"

Ti was off like a flash. Two quick steps and a leap and her small fist grabbed the open jaw. Then the weight came down, dragging the terrorist from the ceiling. The man crashed at Ti's feet, his M-16 still over his shoulder. A quick stomp of the foot into the bent neck gave the goon a lesson in permanent relaxation. Ti took his weapon and ran down the hall, bullets smacking the tile behind her feet.

Being inside the building was not safe now that the terrorists controlled the crawl space. Ti took off for the nearest exit.

CARL LYONS WAS THE FIRST to jump. He grasped the shroud lines and dumped air from one side until he was over the parking lot. Then as he drifted down, all hell broke out on the ground.

There was no mistaking the pale gold of Deborah's hair as she began her sweep of terrorist positions. Lyons could see that he was heading into an ambush. He pulled on the shroud lines, falling faster in a desperate attempt to gain the low flat roof of Elwood Industries. He looked up to make sure that his teammates were following his example. They were. He looked down again and saw Jishin shove Deborah into the open space. He saw bullets cut into her body. He felt his stomach twist, his heart pound. He knew she was dead. He knew the bastards would pay.

Lyons unbuckled the chute and was in motion before his toes touched the roofing tar. Every muzzle-flash that had contributed to the decimation of Deborah Devine was etched permanently on Lyons's tormented mind. He unslung the Atchisson automatic Assault shotgun and jammed home a thirty-round drum. By the time the first round was chambered, the automatic-rifle fire was beginning to zero in on the roof. If Deborah had not furnished such a demanding distraction, Able Team would have been chopped to pieces in the air.

Lyons crouchwalked to the edge of the roof. Each muzzle-flash was answered with a boom from the assault shotgun. Each boom resulted in one bloody death.

Pol and Gadgets landed safely twenty seconds after Lyons. They threw themselves on the flat roof and methodically picked off the terrorists on Lyons's flanks.

When Lyons reached the edge of the roof, he kept walking. The ten-foot drop to the hard surface of the parking lot pounded him less than the jolts he had been receiving from the low-altitude parachute jumps. He automatically flexed his knees, unaware of any shock he was absorbing.

ONE DOES NOT BECOME a successful terrorist by fighting on an equal or near-equal basis. Terrorism is a matter of destroying the defenseless. Aya Jishin understood this very well. When she saw the terror returning to her troops, she ordered them to cut through the building and escape. They grouped and made a charge toward the side door nearest the computer room.

The charge took the terrorists directly under Gadgets. He put his Ingram aside and pulled two antipersonnel grenades. He was about to release them into the stampeding killers when Lao Ti emerged from the door, directly in their path.

Gadgets reacted immediately. He tossed the grenades far enough away that the flying bits of wire would not affect Ti. The double blast shredded terrorist backs but killed none. They were still shook up from the blast when Gadgets landed among them.

The Ingram was meant for close fighting. A wide sweeping burst felled several killers. Gadgets then dropped the weapon because he did not have time to reload and charged those remaining terrorists with Gerber Marks in each hand.

LYONS HEARD THE disturbance and stode toward it. He had seen the desperate dash of the terrorists and Jishin carefully commanding from the center of the mob. She was the one responsible for Deborah's death.

He wanted her.

Politician leaped from the roof. He ran quickly to cover Lyons's back. He knew Ironman was not even thinking about his own back. Politician launched a grenade into a group of terrorists behind Lyons. Those that the grenade did not get, .223 tumblers did.

TI TOOK IN THE situation as soon as she blundered into it. She had more than a dozen terrorists at her back and she could not retreat back to the building. When the blast hit and Gadgets dropped like a gift from the gods, she doubled her effort.

Jishin slipped out of the crowd and tried to circumvent the fight in order to gain the safety of the building. Ti stepped in front of her. Jishin exploded into action, flying at the cause of her defeat, snapping punches and kicks.

Ti backed slowly, concentrating on Jishin, now oblivious to the bullets that began to fly through the open door toward her back.

LYONS REACHED THE group. He saw Jishin and wanted her dead so badly he could feel the ache in his bones. But bullets were coming from the open door. Ti's back had to be covered. Gadgets was also open to the field of fire as he battled hand to hand with the few terrorists left standing outside the building.

Lyons leaped, placing his body between Ti and the flying bullets. The big Atchisson filled the doorway with a storm of death. Terrorists screamed and fell back.

Lyons waded through the door, aiming and shooting, aiming and shooting. No one escaped Death's cold clutch.

A rifle barrel peeked from the ceiling. Two blasts of the big Atchisson added holes to the sound tile, which slowly turned red.

LAO TI CAUGHT Jishin's flashing fist and twisted. This move brought her to face Gadgets's back. She saw he was about to be cleaved by a terrorist knife. She wrenched Jishin's wrist upward, snapping it, then dived at the goon holding the knife. She buried her fist into the man's kidneys. He screamed and twisted, his knife arcing on a path to cross Ti's throat.

Jishin seized the opportunity and ran.

Ti bent backward and avoided the blade. Then she snapped a kick that broke the knife wielder's arm. Gadgets straightened from his final kill and dove a knife into the terrorist's back. The man collapsed like a house of cards.

LYONS EMERGED from the building.

He saw the retreating figure of Jishin.

He saw the bullet-torn body of Deborah Devine.

He saw *red*.

He fired.

Boom!

Mack Bolan's

ABLE TEAM

by Dick Stivers

Action writhes in the reader's own street as Able Team's Carl "Mr. Ironman" Lyons, Pol Blancanales and Gadgets Schwarz make triple trouble in blazing war. To these superspecialists, justice is as sharp as a knife. Join the guys who began it all—Dick Stivers's Able Team!

"This guy has a fertile mind and a great eye for detail. Dick Stivers is brilliant!"

—*Don Pendleton*

Able Team titles are available wherever paperbacks are sold.

GOLD
EAGLE

Mack Bolan's

PHOENIX FORCE

by Gar Wilson

Schooled in guerilla warfare, equipped with all the latest lethal hardware, Phoenix Force battles the powers of darkness in an endless crusade for freedom, justice and the rights of the individual. Follow the adventures of one of the legends of the genre. Phoenix Force is the free world's foreign legion!

"Gar Wilson is excellent! Raw action attacks the reader on every page."

—*Don Pendleton*

GOLD EAGLE

Phoenix Force titles are available wherever paperbacks are sold.

DON PENDLETON'S EXECUTIONER
MACK BOLAN

Sergeant Mercy in Nam . . . The Executioner in the Mafia
Wars . . . Colonel John Phoenix in the Terrorist Wars . . . .
Now Mack Bolan fights his loneliest war! You've never
read writing like this before. Faceless dogsoldiers have
killed April Rose. The Executioner's one link with com-
passion is broken. His path is clear: by fire and maneu-
ver, he will rack up hell in a world shock-tilted by terror.
Bolan wages unsanctioned war—everywhere!

GOLD
EAGLE

HE'S EXPLOSIVE.
HE'S UNSTOPPABLE.
HE'S MACK BOLAN!

He learned his deadly skills in Vietnam...then put them to good use by destroying the Mafia in a blazing one-man war. Now **Mack Bolan** ventures farther into the cold to take on his deadliest challenge yet—the KGB's worldwide terror machine.

Follow the lone warrior on his exciting new missions...and get ready for more nonstop action from his high-powered combat teams: **Able Team**—Bolan's famous Death Squad—battling urban savagery too brutal and volatile for regular law enforcement. And **Phoenix Force**—five extraordinary warriors handpicked by Bolan to fight the dirtiest of antiterrorist wars, blazing into even greater danger.

Fight alongside these three courageous forces for freedom in all-new action-packed novels! Travel to the gloomy depths of the cold Atlantic, the scorching sands of the Sahara, and the desolate Russian plains. You'll feel the pressure and excitement building page after page, with nonstop action that keeps you enthralled until the explosive conclusion!

Now you can have all the new Gold Eagle novels delivered right to your home!

You won't want to miss a single one of these exciting new action-adventures. And you don't have to! Just fill out and mail the card at right, and we'll enter your name in the Gold Eagle home subscription plan. You'll then receive four brand-new action-packed books in the Gold Eagle series every other month, delivered right to your home! You'll get two **Mack Bolan** novels, one **Able Team** book and one **Phoenix Force**. No need to worry about sellouts at the bookstore...you'll receive the latest books by mail as soon as they come off the presses. That's four enthralling action novels every other month, featuring all three of the exciting series included in the Gold Eagle library. Mail the card today to start your adventure.

FREE! Mack Bolan bumper sticker.

When we receive your card we'll send your four explosive Gold Eagle novels and, absolutely FREE, a Mack Bolan "Live Large" bumper sticker! This large, colorful bumper sticker will look great on your car, your bulletin board, or anywhere else you want people to know that you like to "live large." And you are under no obligation to buy anything—because your first four books come on a 10-day free trial! If you're not thrilled with these four exciting books, just return them to us and you'll owe nothing. The bumper sticker is yours to keep, FREE!

Don't miss a single one of these thrilling novels...mail the card now, while you're thinking about it. And get the Mack Bolan bumper sticker FREE as our gift!

BOLAN FIGHTS AGAINST ALL ODDS TO DEFEND FREEDOM

Mail this coupon today!

Gold Eagle Reader Service, a division of Worldwide Library
In U.S.A.: 2504 W. Southern Avenue, Tempe, Arizona 85282
In Canada: P.O. Box 2800, Postal Station 'A', 5170 Yonge Street, Willowdale
Ont. M2N 5T5

FREE! MACK BOLAN BUMPER STICKER
when you join our home subscription plan.

YES, please send me my first four Gold Eagle novels, and include my FREE Mack Bolan bumper sticker as a gift. These first four books are mine to examine free for 10 days. If I am not entirely satisfied with these books, I will return them within 10 days and owe nothing. If I decide to keep these novels, I will pay just $1.95 per book (total $7.80). I will then receive the four new Gold Eagle novels every other month as soon as they come off the presses, and will be billed the same low price of $7.80 per shipment. I understand that each shipment will contain two Mack Bolan novels, one Able Team and one Phoenix Force. There are no shipping and handling or any other hidden charges. I may cancel this arrangement at any time and the bumper sticker is mine to keep as a FREE gift, even if I do not buy any additional books.

166-BPM-PADX

NAME   (PLEASE PRINT)

ADDRESS   APT. NO

CITY   STATE/PROV.   ZIP/POSTAL COD

Signature   (If under 18, parent or guardian must sign.)

This offer limited to one order per household. We reserve the right to exercise discretion in granting membership. If price changes are necessary, you will be notified.
Offer expires October 31, 1984

MB-SUB-